"...Michael Gear has transformed America's obses-
sion with Hollywood beauty into an epic thriller of
transcendent terror. I thought the world would
come to an end with comet strikes, mushroom
clouds, and apocalyptic plagues. I never dreamed
we'd overwhelm the earth with J-Lo look-alikes and
George Clooney clones."

— JACK ANDERSON, PULITZER PRIZE-
WINNING JOURNALIST

"With a Crichton-like mix of scientific intrigue and
pulse-pounding suspense, the Gears deliver a fasci-
nating exploration of the frontiers of science."

— BOOKLIST ON RAISING ABEL

"Gear writes superbly rolling prose with flair, confi-
dence, wit, an ear for sounds, and an eye for details
.... And he has another gift: the ability to teach his
readers as he entertains them."

— ROCKY MOUNTAIN NEWS ON THE
MORNING RIVER

# ATHENA UNLEASHED

# Also by W. Michael Gear

*Big Horn Legacy*

*Dark Inheritance*

*The Foundation*

*Fracture Event*

*Long Ride Home*

*Raising Abel*

Flight of the Hawk Series

The Moundville Duology

The Wyoming Chronicles

Saga of a Mountain Sage Series

The Anasazi Mysteries

The Athena Trilogy

# ATHENA UNLEASHED
## THE ATHENA TRILOGY PART ONE

W. MICHAEL GEAR

WOLFPACK
PUBLISHING
— EST 2013 —

Wolfpack Publishing
9850 S. Maryland Parkway, Suite A-5 #323
Las Vegas, Nevada 89183

wolfpackpublishing.com

This book is a work of fiction. Any references to historical events, real people or real places are used fictitiously. Other names, characters, places and events are products of the author's imagination, and any resemblance to actual events, places or persons, living or dead, is entirely coincidental.

Paperback ISBN 978-1-63977-248-3
eBook ISBN 978-1-63977-247-6

*To Jim and "Tuck" Mills*
*in hopes that the joy of the hunt forever fills your hearts.*

# Acknowledgments

The Athena Trilogy was written with the help and encouragement of John Meyer, Jr., Vice President of sales and the international training division at Heckler & Koch in Sterling, Virginia. John graciously allowed us to participate in the elite HK Executive Protection course. Additional appreciation is extended to Patsy Drew-Rios, Forrest "Skip" Carroll, Bob Schneider, Tom Taylor, and the 9-02 Executive Training class; thank you all for indulging an amateur among professionals. If the books succeed, it is due to your intense and comprehensive training.

A novel isn't created in a vacuum. Half of this work is Kathleen O'Neal Gear's.

# ATHENA UNLEASHED

# PROLOGUE

That morning, Gregor McEwan was faced with two of his greatest hatreds: He hated to rush. He hated hangovers even more. A bottle of orange juice, followed by a breakfast of rashers, toast and jam, and cheddar-laced eggs had taken neither the edge off his quaking nerves nor the quiver out of his rebellious stomach. They had, however, dulled the sour taste of undigested red ale that still cloyed the back of his tongue.

Nothing would cut the headache but time.

The clock showed half seven, and given the thick fog hanging beyond the window, his normal forty-five-minute commute to the lab would be doubled.

Gregor stopped in the hallway. There he donned his wool coat and looked at the plaque hung prominently on the wall.

TO GREGOR A. McEWAN
OUR BRIGHTEST STAR
FOR OUTSTANDING LEADERSHIP
Q-GEN LABORATORIES

Beside it was a framed glossy photo showing Gregor wearing a tweed jacket, narrow dark-blue tie, and pressed trousers. For once, his sandy hair had been combed, and the blaze of superiority in his dark brown eyes had been fairly won. Gregor liked his face in the photo. The lighting was just right for his smooth-shaven cheeks with a handsome combination of angles over a strong chin. Beside him at the podium stood Q-Gen's president, Calvin Fowler. Fowler was presenting Gregor a check along with the plaque. They were smiling at the camera, plaque in one hand, check in the other. Gregor thought they looked like the sort of self-congratulatory politicians who concocted flawed Middle Eastern peace accords.

Gregor, a PhD two years out of Cambridge, had just turned twenty-nine, and despite his youth, had become the most successful team leader at Q-Gen.

Not that he wasn't without faults. He had serious failings when it came to both women and full-bodied ales. As had been the case last night when Beatrice stood him up at the Chop and Ale. Spurned by one, he had overindulged in the other.

Which was why he felt miserable, hungover, and was late to work. Not that it actually mattered in the grand scheme of things. He had no peers at Q-Gen when it came to coaxing zygotes to begin that initial stage of division that led to a viable embryo. He rarely put in less than a sixty-hour week. So even if he was a wee bit late on occasion, nothing would be said by his superiors.

Gregor didn't mind that his colleagues called him a prick. Given his recent successes in nuclear DNA extraction while maintaining cytoplasmic integrity, he could find work in any laboratory in the world. At that very moment, he and his team were drafting a seminal paper for publication in the prestigious journal *Nature* that would revolutionize the biotech world the way Wilmut and Campbell had done with Dolly the sheep.

The key was in avoiding cellular disturbance as the large mass of nuclear DNA was extracted and replaced. The more the organelles—the working structures inside the cell—were disturbed, the less likely the chance for success.

Dolly, it turned out, had been a miracle. Given the techniques of the time, her creation had been the equivalent of brain surgery accomplished with a stone axe. Gregor and his Q-Gen team were taking the manipulation of reproductive science in totally new directions.

Assuming his head didn't split from the damned hangover and kill him first.

"The price of greatness," he told his reflection. Then winked at himself, just for good luck. He reached down for his briefcase where it sat by his rubber boots and plucked his wool cap from its peg before opening the door.

The morning smelled cool and damp. Thick gray fog softened the lines of his hedgerow and the trellised gate that let out onto the road. He turned right, following the stepping stones embedded in his uncut grass to his old green Jaguar. Skid marks in the gravel marked where the car had slewed to a stop mere inches from a cock-up.

Gregor winced, glancing suspiciously at the body. Water beaded and trickled in round droplets from the waxed surface, but no dents or scrapes marred the sleek metal.

It appeared he hadn't hit anything on the way home. Thank God for that. He'd been lucky again.

"Have to stop that shit," he muttered as he walked up to the driver's door and fished keys from his pocket. He lifted the lever, surprised to find it locked.

He never locked the car here, so far out in the country. Using his fingers, he slicked the dampness from the glass to see the lock was down. He squinted at his key fob. Pressing the right button, the locks clicked up.

"Bloody hell." He squinted against the pain in his head, endured the sudden queasiness that tightened around his breakfast and made his mouth water. He pressed his eyes closed, willing the sickness away.

When he finally opened them, two men had stepped up to take positions on either side of him. As if they had magically popped out of the fog.

He jumped, startled, whirling about and stammering, "Who're you? Damn! Gave me a start, you did."

"Dr. McEwan," the man to his right said with an accented voice. "We are sorry to bother you."

Gregor peered past the lowered brim of the man's dew-silvered wool cap, seeing intense black eyes and a thin hooked nose above a severe mouth. He looked Arab or Persian, his right hand balled in the coat's large pocket.

The companion had a thickset body with powerful shoulders and a similar, if broader, face atop a hard jaw. They both wore long waxed-cloth jackets over denim pants. Heavy hiking boots, dark with dew, impressed patterns into the gravel.

"Right, right." Gregor recovered, one hand to his heart. "Look, I'm running bloody late. Whatever it is, can it wait until later? My number's in the book. Ring me up or leave a message on the machine."

"We hate to bother," the first man repeated, stepping close. His hand slipped free of the pocket. Gregor blinked—his mind stumbling over the reality of the sleek black pistol pointed at his navel.

"Shit!" Was that a real gun? "Look, I don't know what this is about, but if I did something last night, I bloody well apologize. I'll make it square, whatever it was. Honest, you don't have to go to extremes, right?"

"You will come with us." The second man's voice had a harsh raspy quality.

"It is not what you have done," the first rejoined. "It is what you *will* do. Hold still. This will hurt only a little."

From the corner of his eye, Gregor caught the second man's quick movement. Arms, strong as steel bands, tightened around him. His briefcase gave a hollow thunk as it fell to the gravel.

"I..." Gregor never finished. The first man stepped close, the pistol jamming into Gregor's stomach. For an instant their eyes held—remorseless inevitability behind the Arab's. The man's other hand rose. Gregor caught a glimpse of the needle: a filament on the syringe. A sharp sting was followed by a cool rush into the side of his neck.

Gregor opened his mouth to scream, but the pistol speared hard under his solar plexus.

*Dear God! What's happening to me?*

This couldn't be! Not to him! He was a scientist, for God's sake! It wasn't possible. It just wasn't...

His last memory was of those hard black eyes dropping away into eternity.

---

## WOODLAND, CALIFORNIA

The black minute hand pointed at the ten, and the thick hour hand had crept way past the eleven. Nancy Hartlee arched her back as she studied the clock. The lab was cluttered with tubes and tube racks, rows of micropipettes, several microscopes, different sizes of centrifuges and electrophoresis gel trays with wires running to the power supplies, two transilluminators, a PCR machine, and a big hood next to the autoclave. It all looked stark under the white fluorescent light.

Nancy had passed her twenty-seventh birthday two days ago. Had missed any and all celebration. Something about being unable to fit it into her twenty-hour days. When at work she kept her shoulder-length brown hair pulled back in a ponytail. Green eyes and a delicate nose didn't quite balance the strong jaw and sharp cheeks. She wasn't homely, just different. Oddly, men thought her attractive, mostly because of the poise and the natural grace with which she carried herself. Swimming had been her passion during her high school years; she had the state championship medals on her wall to prove it.

She'd been in the lab for sixteen intense hours. No wonder her whole body ached, and she couldn't think straight. Stretching didn't seem to help the cramps in her back. Twelve hours ago, she'd seen the clock hands in the same position—but that had been just before she, Mark, and Jim had walked down the hall, out to the parking lot, and bought warm burritos from the canteen van.

"Hey," Nancy called as she returned her attention to the micrographs on the light table. "What's the verdict?"

Jim poked his head around the lab door and replied, "We're there! Mark just placed the last tray in the incubator. As far as we can tell, everything's okay." He grinned. "Cool, huh?"

"Great. Button up and get the hell out of here. If you hurry, you can still make it before midnight." She gave him a meaningful nod. "*Just* before midnight."

She rubbed her tired eyes and walked back to her little cubicle of an office. The light's white glow ate right through her into her brain. She closed her eyes for a moment's respite. When she blinked them open again, the world was maddeningly just the way she'd left it.

She slid into her chair, rolled in front of the computer, and began tapping in her notes. Seventeen of their twenty specimens were positive and ready for implantation. The oocytes had been interrupted at the second meiosis, the point where the maternal chromosomes were duplicated and separated. In that state, her team had incised the cellular wall with their latest generation nano scalpel and carefully removed the nuclear DNA through a process called enucleation.

Nanotechnology was their prize. Nancy had always believed that many of the problems in reliably cloning mammals lay in the manner in which nuclear DNA was removed and reinserted into the host oocyte. Their nano scalpel sliced through the plasma membrane, the vitelline space, and the zona pellucida instead of punching through them with all the finesse of a blunt-nosed bullet the way the older pipettes did.

Then nuclear DNA from a donor—for ethical reasons Nancy had used her own—had been inserted. The cytoplasm, the liquid soup of cellular function, was comprehensively monitored for minute changes in chemistry. Rumor had it that Q-Gen was way ahead of her team when it came to that. Let them be. She had the nano scalpel.

Nancy recorded the last of her observations as Mark called, "Good night. See you when?"

"Take tomorrow off. Sleep. Rest. Recharge your batteries."

"Cool! Good night."

She turned back to the screen and frowned. They had been sure that the key to a viable clone lay in the cytoplasm and the orientation of the inserted nuclear DNA. Cellular trauma and disruption to the organelles, especially the endoplasmic reticulum, had to be mini-mized; the nuclear DNA had to be placed in just the right position to ensure the embryo's correct development.

Finishing her notes, she smiled up at the picture over her desk. There, a bright-eyed baby chimp lay cuddled in its mother's arms. Her first triumph.

Nancy saved her work, backed it up, and put the computer into sleep mode before she found her purse and walked to the door. Flipping off the lights, she locked up, set the security system, and yawned as she tottered down the hall. The fifteen-minute drive to her apartment was going to feel interminable.

Nevertheless, as she stepped out into the cool California night, she experienced a sense of exhilaration. If they had seventeen viable embryos out of twenty, they had beaten the odds. She was already composing the article for *Science* in her head.

Three vehicles were left in the lot. The security guy's Ford pickup was off in the corner, and an unfamiliar Excursion gleamed in the spot beside her battered Toyota. Had someone gotten a new SUV? And such a monster, at that?

Her tired mind dismissed it as she walked between the vehicles and bent to insert her key into the lock.

The soft click of a door behind her was the only warning.

It came much too late.

---

ECHUNGA FARMS, NEAR ADELAIDE, SOUTH AUSTRALIA

Brian Everly kicked manure from his rubber overshoes and climbed the cement steps to the farm office. Echunga Farms Ltd. had a large complex of paddocks and hay barns with a tool shed and mechanical building for the storage of tractors and loaders.

Brian's four-door Holden sedan was parked on the other side of the fence next to a hay wagon. He could see heat waves on the bonnet as the faded brown paint baked in the hot sun.

He opened the office door, slipped off his overshoes, and stepped inside.

Clairice Higgins sat at the desk. She looked up and arched an inquisitive eyebrow. She was in her forties, gray-haired, with a round face used to smiling. Too many years in the Aussie sun had faded her blue eyes and taken its toll on her wrinkling skin.

Brian smiled. "All three of the lambs are doing well. No signs of any abnormality. The vet just left with blood and urine specimens to run at university, but I think they're doing brilliantly."

"And the celebrities?" she asked.

Brian turned slightly so he could look out the window at the "wolf" building. This wasn't a real wolf, but the once-extinct marsupial wolf, *Thylacinus cynocephalus*. A predator native to Australia before the arrival of the Europeans. Brian liked to say "once-extinct" because now two immature females were exploring the hay out in the wolf building. The third, a little male, had just begun peeking out of Bertha's pouch. Bertha was a matronly, if somewhat foul-tempered, giant red kangaroo. Her uteri had been host to "Beth" the first wolf, and then "Gina" and "Max" in sequence.

Clairice didn't jest when she called them celebrities. ABC, BBC, and a slew of American, French, and Japanese media had paraded through the farm when Beth was first born.

Echunga Farms had been host to the first successful resurrection of an extinct species. Brian, working in a postdoctoral position, had succeeded where so many had failed. Not just once, but with three different embryos created from three different museum-derived donor specimens. He was waiting for the patent to be registered before he authored his first refereed paper on the methodology.

"Max is a terror," Brian replied. "I'm afraid if he bites Bertha one more time, she's going to boot him right through the wall."

"So, the vet says they're healthy?" Clairice lifted an eyebrow. "I've got to phone in to the ABC in Melbourne, you know. They want weekly reports. A bit of Aussie pride, right? We *were* the first."

Brian sobered. "I wish they wouldn't be so bloody sure of themselves. It is a first. I keep reminding people of that. They have forgotten that we only got three successes out of four hundred and six attempts. So much can still go wrong. It's like being in the red center, right? We don't know where we're at, or if there's even water at the end of the road. It's damned easy to get lost when you're a trailblazer."

Clairice reached for her glasses, rubbed them on her blue cotton skirt, and slipped them on. "All I need to say is that they are still alive and healthy. One day at a time."

"Right. I'm out of here. I have a meeting this afternoon at the agricultural station. Martin wants to go over some figures, and then it's off to the solicitor."

"Price of success. Drive carefully," Clairice added as she returned her attention to the papers on her desk.

Brian walked through the office and out the front door. He followed the cement walk to his Holden and slipped into the driver's seat. The vinyl on the dash was cracked, the steering wheel warm under his hands. The car smelled old and dusty in the hot air.

The engine ground, squealed, and roared to life when Brian turned the key. He grasped the shift lever with his left hand, slipping it into reverse. Once he had backed around the hay wagon he followed the road out. At the security gate, the guard waved while the chain-link gate rumbled open.

Brian turned onto the blacktop and ran through the gears. Someday soon, when the paperwork was done and his process licensed, he'd have enough for a nice car. Maybe a Lexus or top-line Toyota.

Winding along the banks of Echunga Creek, he passed manicured farms alternating with virgin patches of eucalyptus trees. He slowed, downshifting as he approached the intersection. A man was standing beside the stop sign where the road T'd at Mt. Bold Reservoir. To Brian's surprise, the fellow waved and stepped over as the Holden's squeaking brakes brought the vehicle to a stop.

"Dr. Everly?" The man leaned down, smiling into the window. He wore a brown Akubra hat, a light canvas jacket, and a shirt open at the collar. Something about him, the dark thin features, spurred the briefest of warnings.

"Yes, but I can't chat now. Please, call my office, and they will be most happy to—" The thin black pistol was centered between Brian's eyes.

"Do not move, Dr. Everly," the man's accented voice cooed. "Do not try to drive off. It will only get you killed."

Stunned, wordless, Brian was barely aware of the second man who walked up on the car's offside. It took all of his will to glance away from the gun when the door clicked open. A big man—also Arab-looking—had settled into the passenger seat to his left.

"You will follow my friend's instructions, Doctor, and you will not be hurt." The gunman smiled as he opened the rear door and slipped into the seat. "On the contrary, we want you to be very, very healthy."

# CHAPTER I

The carpeted hallway was empty. Lymon
Bridges double-checked to make sure as he
stepped out of Sheela Marks' plush penthouse suite. He glanced up and down from long habit,
checking for potential threats, and found none.

He turned, nodded to Dot McGuire—Sheela's
publicist—and waited while she and Sheela Marks
stepped outside. Sheela clutched her fake gold-plated
plastic Oscar statue in her manicured hands. She was
holding it upside down like a misshapen kitchen knife.
Dot, in her midforties, walked behind in a tweed jacket
and gray skirt.

Sheela was resplendent. Dot had dressed her in a
sheer silvery sheath by Dolce and Gabbana that glistened with each step. It also accented the sensual
curves of her hip and bust. She wore white michelle K
stilettos that gave her another five inches—as if she

needed them—and a white furry Dior boa wrapped around her shoulders. Her hair appeared immaculate, piled up on top with long reddish-blond locks falling down her back. The entire image was to remind people that she'd won the Oscar last month for her performance in *Blood Rage*.

A quick glance behind assured Lymon that both Dot and Sheela were following as he led the way to the service elevator. Lymon liked the St. Regis. They were used to the needs of security and capable of lodging prominent people with their demanding requirements. Lymon lifted his left cuff, saying, "We're on the way to the elevator."

*"Roger,"* Paul's voice assured in his earpiece. *"We're go. Limo's at the Door Three curb."*

Sheela asked Dot, "God, are we still on for that thing in Atlanta? I mean, we're two weeks into the promotion, the box office is down fifteen million from last week. What does the studio expect? That CNN can bring us back up? The buzz is on Chris Pine and his robot revenge flick now."

"Just do it," Dot chided. "You know the game. So does the studio, and so, too, does CNN. No sense in pissing them off with a no-show. Face time never hurts. Not for this box office and not for the next. Not to mention the social media bump we'll get. Yahoo and Apple will pick it up. It's just one more day."

"And another hotel, and another airplane, and another room-service meal." Sheela's face pained. "No, I'll be honest. Here's what I really hate: It's the same damn questions that I've been answering for the last three weeks."

Her voice dropped to a journalist's slightly superior

lilt. " 'What's it like to work with Tom Samson?' 'Have you been seeing anyone since you broke up with de Giulio?' 'What is your next project?' 'What's *Jagged Cat* about?' 'Who stars?' Over and over and over again. Dot, can't we just send them the clips?"

Lymon's lips twitched at the note of frustration. Hey, it was the modern reality. Back in the good old days, actors didn't have to globe-trot to build hype for a picture. Then COVID gave them a break. As did the SAG strike. Firms like his could consist of one to four guys and cover everything. Now people in his business had to be like a mini secret service, employing enough coverage to ensure a client's protection around the globe.

The elevator dinged, and Lymon positioned himself. As the doors opened, he blocked Sheela's body with his own until satisfied that the cage was empty. He held the door as they entered and placed himself to repulse anyone who might try to slip in at the last instant. Only then did he press the button for the first floor.

"Zemeckis is throwing a party Friday night," Sheela reminded. "It would be good exposure for us. Universal and DreamWorks are going to be there."

"Rex knows that." Dot frowned. "Look, we can do both. I'll talk to the producer at CNN, see if they can tape early. That means we fly in, shuttle to CNN Plaza, shoot the piece, and have you on the plane back to LA. Weather, CNN personnel, and the FAA permitting, you're at Zemeckis' by seven. Eight at the latest." She turned to Lymon. "Can you do that? Find us a jet back to LA on such short notice?"

"Shouldn't be a problem," Lymon answered,

mentally noting that he'd be on the phone to the Am-Ex Centurion travel service while Sheela was on camera.

The elevator slowed, settled, and stopped. Lymon was ready when the door opened and stepped out in a blocking stance. The hall was clear. He gave the briefest of nods and stepped in slightly behind Sheela's left shoulder as she started toward the door. The hallway wasn't long, no more than forty feet to the fire exit. He nodded at the security camera over the door. Hotel security had been notified of their route and supposedly were watching.

Past that last metal door, he had fifteen feet to the curb, and Paul would have the limo door unlocked for him to open.

"We're in the hallway," Lymon said into the sleeve mic.

*"Roger,"* Paul returned. *"Sidewalk's clear. No visible threats."*

Routine.

The word had no more than formed in Lymon's head when a door opened to the right. A man stepped out.

Instinct led Lymon to take a half-step forward. In that brief moment he took the guy's measure: medium height, dark complexion, Middle Eastern or maybe Mexican, muscular and clean-shaven. The guy was dressed in the hotel's bellstand uniform. He was holding something in each hand that Lymon couldn't see. The man jerked a short but polite nod, the sort staff were supposed to give guests, and said, "Good day."

Lymon was stepping past him when their eyes met.

It was something feral, excited—something that shouldn't have been in a hotel guy's eyes.

Lymon was moving to block him when the guy lunged at Sheela.

Lymon's arm caught the guy's chest, spinning him slightly off balance. He could feel the muscle, the athletic charge in the man's tensed body. One of the assailant's arms flashed up, the elbow catching Lymon on the cheek like a pile driver, batting him hard. The other shot out for Sheela.

It was the briefest glimpse: something glass or clear plastic, capped in blue with a needle tipping it. The attacker's arm had thrust out like a fencer's, lancing the device at Sheela.

Lymon would remember the expression on her face, the look of shock in her eyes, as she stumbled backward, away from the assault.

Lymon caught his balance, planted a foot, and ducked under the outstretched arm. He jabbed with his own elbow, striking at the man's ribs. That quickly, the assailant twisted away and his other hand rose, a blocky black thing clutched there. He jabbed it at Lymon's side.

The jolt sent a spasm through Lymon's body; lightning flashed behind his eyes. Convulsing, he bucked backward into Sheela.

Dot was screaming at the top of her lungs. Lymon could hear Sheela's panicked gasp as she struggled under his weight.

The bellhop hesitated, a desperate expression on his face. Lymon caught his breath, willed his body to react, and bulled his way forward on rubbery muscles as Sheela pushed him from behind.

The bellhop dug in a pocket and pulled something —an aluminum can—free. Lymon saw the man's thumb as it popped a ring up. The guy dropped the can before turning to run.

*Catch the son of a bitch!*

It took all of his self-control to hesitate. The gleaming aluminum canister was hissing as it rolled along the carpet. Dot was still screaming something unintelligible. Sheela looked like a spotlighted deer.

Lymon turned, bent, and drove his body into Sheela's, tumbling her backward and bowling Dot off her feet. The fake Oscar statue bounced across the carpet.

"Stay down!" he screamed as he threw himself on top of Sheela's squirming body. "Don't move!"

He stared into her terror-bright eyes, was aware of her open mouth, of her tongue so pink behind perfect white teeth.

*Bang!* Lightning strobed, blinding in intensity. Lymon's body jerked at the concussion, and something slapped painfully through his skull. He winced, cringed, and tried to press Sheela's body into his own. His ears hurt and rang— the way they did when someone shot a large-caliber handgun in a small room.

He could feel Sheela's body, looked into her famous blue eyes, and watched her panic. Later, he would remember the pulse throbbing in her neck.

It seemed an eternity before he felt the hand on his shoulder, turned his head, and looked up. Paul was leaning down, his lips moving as if shouting, but only the horrible ringing filled Lymon's ears.

*Dear God! What just happened here?*

# CHAPTER 2

FBI HEADQUARTERS, PENNSYLVANIA AVENUE,
WASHINGTON, D.C.

The clicking of the pen was slowly driving Special Agent Christal Anaya toward lethal violence. She was sitting next to Sid Harness —maybe her last friend in the world—and he kept clicking the damned ballpoint with his thumb. She was in enough trouble—her career balanced on the line. At best, she faced professional humiliation, at worst, outright dismissal. Nevertheless, it took every fiber of being and will to keep from reaching out, twisting the pen out of Sid's hand, and driving it into his neck like a stiletto.

The conference room was on the seventh floor, mucky-muck territory where the suits lived. It had taken extraordinary measures to bring Christal here. Measures so extreme that she had drawn the personal attention of the assistant director himself. The man sat at the far end of the polished mahogany table, armed with a yellow legal pad, a cup of coffee, and a stack of reports that outlined both the salient and sordid facts that had brought Christal to this room.

To the AD's right sat Special Agent in Charge Peter Wirthing, from the Washington Metro Field Office. To his right was Hank Abrams, agent in charge of the WMFO's RICO team, and the cause of Christal's current dilemma. Not once since she had taken a seat had the filthy *cabron* even dared to look her in the eyes.

She was seeing an entirely different side of Hank Abrams now. How could a man who had been so on top of things, so in charge, have collapsed into this dripping *menudo*?

"Agent Anaya," Wirthing said after meeting the AD's cool gray eyes. "We have reviewed every aspect of this current situation. Until the unfortunate incident in the surveillance van, we couldn't have asked for more. Your work had been exemplary. Everything was falling into place." He looked down at the stack of glossy photos on the table in front of him. "After having received these, however, I'm afraid that we're going to have to drop our case against Gonzales."

Bill Smart, the federal prosecutor who sat at the AD's left, nodded, looking down the table, past Sid and into Christal's eyes. "The fact is, the case is blown. After Gonzales got his hands on those"—he indicated the photos—"we haven't got a chance in hell of getting a conviction."

"In short," Wirthing said flatly, "everything we've worked toward for a year and a half has just flown out the window." His hard brown eyes met hers. "Bye-bye."

It was the way he said it. She swallowed hard, glancing at Hank. He just sat there, head down, eyes on his hands where they were clasped before him on the table. She could see sweat beading on his forehead. He looked like a man awaiting the gallows. A penitent who had been condemned in spite of his late-found piety and prayers.

She, however, refused to play that game. She kept her head up, glaring angrily. At least on the outside. Inside she felt like someone had taken a weed eater to her guts. The sick feeling, like she was going to throw up, just got worse.

"Agent Anaya, if you would excuse us for a moment?" the assistant director said.

When she didn't move, he nodded irritably toward the door.

Christal tensed, nodded, and said, "Yes. Of course." She glanced miserably at Hank, but he just sat there, a whipped puppy, staring at his sweaty hands.

Thankfully, her legs didn't betray her on that walk to the door. When she grasped the knob and opened it, she looked back. All eyes but Hank's were on her, seeing what? The woman she was in the photos? Comparing them to her now?

Face rigid, she stepped out into the empty hallway, crossed her arms, and rubbed her hands up and down the sleeves of her gray wool suit coat. Having nothing else to do, she studied the faces on the portraits hanging from the walls. Dead white men. All of them. Smiling, gray-haired, looking old and fat, like cats who had lived out of the can for so long they had forgotten how to hunt.

*How did it come to this?*

She tried to think past the gloom and disbelief that clouded her mind. The last couple of days had been one shock after another. It had all begun the first time she had seen the photos.

*How did they do it? How did they get them?*

The *why* wasn't an issue. With them, Enrique Gonzales destroyed any chance the government had of prosecution. No grand jury on earth would indict. The slime was going to walk. Because of her and Hank, and what they'd done in the van that night. *Shit!*

She might have been standing there for an eternity. Or was it just seconds before Sid stepped out and walked over? He stopped beside her, staring at the same portrait. He was antsy, rocking from his toes to his heels.

"So?" she asked softly.

He cleared his throat. "They think it would be best if you simply offered your resignation."

"And Hank?"

"He'll be taken care of."

"What?" she cried, whirling to stare. "Taken care of in *what* way?"

Sid looked like he'd just eaten something covered with fuzzy gray mold. "Demotion. Transfer to North Dakota or some such thing."

"Hey! He was *half* of it! That's his white butt sticking up in those photos! What do they think? That I *raped* him? Huh? That I manipulated him?"

"Hey, Christal," Sid pleaded, "I know how it looks, but listen—"

"Listen, hell! These guys are setting themselves up for one hell of an EEO—"

"No!" Sid grabbed her hands, cupping them in his own as he glared down into her hot eyes. "You don't want to play that card. Not even if it's only a threat."

"Why not? I get to resign? Hank gets a slap on the hand? Give me one fucking good reason why I don't file a sexual discrimination suit against those bastards!"

"Because they'll hammer you. What's it been? Three years that you've been with the Bureau? You know how it works. This isn't some supervisor walking up and grabbing your ass. You and Hank literally screwed up an eighteen-month investigation. A major-league scumball is going to walk away from this without having to pay for what he did or what he's going to keep right on doing. A lot of your fellow agents are going to be *really* pissed about that. Think about the kind of testimony Wirthing can compile. A lot of people are going to look at it as a way of getting back at you, Chris. Even...even old friends."

"You, Sid?"

He smiled sadly. "No. Not me. But I'll feel the heat."

She searched his eyes. "You really mean that, don't you?"

He shrugged. "You know, if I wasn't married—"

"It didn't stop Hank!"

"Yeah. Yeah. Well, you've always had really shitty taste in men."

She felt her soul slip down inside her. "They'd really do that? Go out of their way to destroy me?"

"Put yourself in their shoes. You know they would." Sid licked his lips. "And if you push it all the way to a hearing, you know those photos are going to be exhibit one. Center stage. I don't think you want that. Not if the press gets a hold of it." His eyes pleaded with her.

"Take the easy way out. Fall on your sword. There's life after death."

"And if I fight for my life?"

"They'll see you in hell."

# CHAPTER 3

Paul wheeled the limo off the street into Sheela Marks' drive and hesitated as the security gates rolled open. Lymon, in the passenger seat, waved up at the camera, aware that John, head of the house security detail, was recording their entrance.

"You know," Sheela called from the plush back seat, "I wonder if it's worth it anymore."

"Pardon?" Lymon asked, turning in his seat.

"All this." She waved at the gates as they drove through. "The cameras, the gates and fences, the motion detectors. God, I feel like I'm living in South Africa."

"It will all settle into routine again," Lymon told her. "You've just had a scare. Hell, I'm rattled, too." Thank God the ringing in his ears had finally gone away.

They drove past the gardens and manicured lawn and pulled up in the circular drive before the big house.

Rex's Ferrari and Dot's BMW were already parked off to the side. So was Felix's Bentley. Apparently the life of a Hollywood lawyer wasn't anything to sneeze at. Finally, Tony Zell's BMW Z8 was nosed in next to the rose bushes.

"Everyone's here," Sheela noted, voice a bit off. "Wringing their hands over my health."

Lymon said nothing, but shared a glance with Paul when he stopped the limo in front of the house's arching double doors. The original owner had imported them from a fourteenth-century Spanish cathedral. The wood was black and cracked, hand-hewn out of sections of oak. The things were so heavy they hung on special hinges, and the door frame was a giant steel arch overlaid with stone.

Lymon got out and was reaching for the rear door when Sheela opened it herself. She stepped out wearing one of Marc Jacobs's white cotton blouses, beige Chloe trousers, and had a light cotton Bottega Veneta coat hung over her shoulders. A Fendi leather purse was clutched in her hands. When she gave Lymon a faint smile, a distance lay behind her eyes. "You ready for this?"

Lymon shrugged. "After you, ma'am."

He glanced back when the big limo purred to life. Paul waved, slipped the car into gear, and accelerated around the circle, headed for the garage out back.

Lymon followed Sheela up the steps to the giant doors. As if on cue, the right swung open. Tomaso, head of the household staff, called, "Good to have you home, Ms. Marks."

"Thank you, Tomaso. Are they in the meeting room?"

"They are. Can I get you anything?" He tilted his head inquisitively.

"Sparkling water, thank you." She glanced back at Lymon. "Anything?"

"Coffee, if it wouldn't be too much trouble." It wouldn't, of course. It never was.

Behind Sheela, Lymon padded along on his cushioned shoes, feeling like a lion turned loose in the petting zoo. He barely glanced at the Southwestern artwork hanging on the white stucco walls, or the lacquered bronze sculptures resting in corners and in the hollow beneath the grand staircase. Underfoot, the marble tiles made a faint squishy sound under his rubber soles.

At the end of the hall Sheela made a left, leading him into the meeting room. Fifteen by thirty, the room was paneled in walnut with floor-to-ceiling bookshelves. A sixty-inch TV was built into one wall and attached to a satellite communications center for virtual conferences. A long and splendid maple table dominated the center, while leather-covered chairs with ample stuffing surrounded it. The small wet bar in one corner sported a rack of bottles, a tiny sink, and a built-in refrigerator. Gleaming chandeliers cast soft light on the hard people already seated at the table.

"What the hell happened back there?" Rex demanded before anyone else could speak. He fastened his bulldog eyes on Lymon. Rex Gerber had served as Sheela's manager for the last four years, riding her rising star like a Frontier Days cowboy in a Cheyenne bareback contest. At fifty-eight, he liked to think he was younger than his round belly, balding head, and fleshy nose indicated.

"We were ambushed in the hotel hallway." Lymon spoke professionally, refusing to go for the bait.

"What if he'd had a gun?" the lawyer, Felix Baylor, asked.

Lymon met the man's quick brown eyes. A sharp cookie and noted LA hotshot, Baylor had just turned forty-five. Along with his Bentley, he liked expensive trappings. The guy had a thing about being dressed to the nines; his shoes alone—custom-made Italian from a place on Rodeo Drive—would have paid a year's rent in west LA.

"Well, Felix, he could have killed Sheela, Dot, and me. Fortunately, you'll be happy to know that New York has even stricter gun laws than we do in California, so obviously he had to make do with a needle, a stun gun, and a flash-bang. Right?"

"Shit!" Tony Zell, Sheela's agent, muttered. His fingers were tapping a rhythm on a glass of iced scotch. Tony was blond, tall, blue-eyed, and fit. His thing was flash. He liked gold, be it chains, rings, or watches. When he wasn't doing power lunches, he chose to play tennis or golf. Rumor had it that some kid with dreams of being an actor detailed his Z8 once a day.

"Hey, the guy was in a hotel uniform," Dot shot back. She was sitting at the head of the table and had come dressed casually in a pink skirt, white blouse, and tennis shoes. "I was there. I looked the guy in the face and dismissed him. I still don't know how Lymon acted as fast as he did."

"Are you sure you're okay?" Rex turned to Sheela, rising from his chair.

"I'm fine. Lymon was on the guy," Sheela insisted as she and Lymon took seats.

"What about this needle?" Rex insisted. "Was he trying to inject you with something?"

"We don't know," Lymon said. "Nothing squirted out of it during the scuffle. I just got a glimpse, but it looked as if the plunger was down. I'd say it was empty."

"That's nuts!" Rex cried. "What was he after? Blood drive?"

"Have you given any thought to suing?" Felix asked as he squared his legal pad in front of him.

"Suing?" Lymon asked incredulously.

"It was a hotel uniform." Felix pulled a diamond-studded Montblanc from his pocket; thin white fingers caressed it like a tobaccoholic would a Cuban cigar. "They have responsibilities to their guests, and they obviously tripped all over themselves in Sheela's case. As a result of their negligence, Sheela Marks' life was placed in jeopardy."

"Bullshit!" Lymon shook his head. "So...you thinking about suing me, too?"

No humor lay behind Felix's eyes. "Lymon, we don't know what to think of your actions during the last forty-eight hours."

An old and familiar tightening began in Lymon's chest as his gaze burned into the lawyer's.

"Stop it!" Sheela slapped a hand on the table. "It wasn't Lymon's fault. Or the hotel's. We're not suing anybody."

Rex pushed a folded copy of the *Los Angeles Times* across the table. His thick thumb jabbed at a below-the-fold headline. The slug line read:

QUEEN OF SCREEN ASSAULTED:

A picture of her receiving her Oscar got as much space as the story. From what Lymon could glimpse, it was a rehashing of the police report.

"The hotel couldn't have prevented it," Lymon added softly. "This guy was a pro."

"Huh?" Rex and Felix muttered in unison. Tony had straightened, a quizzical look in his dreamy blue eyes.

"He was too good at his job." Lymon shoved the paper back at Rex. "It wasn't any secret that Sheela was staying at the St. Regis. She had reporters up to the suite for three days before the assault. It didn't take a rocket scientist to figure out her departure time from the hotel. We'd advertised the fact she was doing the *Late Show,* and people know when it tapes. The studio sells tickets, right? Stars generally want to spend as little time as possible in the green room. So that gives the guy about a thirty-minute window to intercept Sheela. The hallway is the perfect choke point. I say the guy is a pro because he worked this out without me seeing him. His surveillance and planning were perfect."

"So he did his homework. That doesn't make him professional." Tony crossed his arms.

"The police never found a print. Everything was either wiped down or smudged. The door he stepped out of was always locked, but when the guy went into that broom closet, he didn't jimmy the lock. He had a key. We watched on the security camera tapes later. He knew his target, knew what he wanted with her, and he damn near got it."

All eyes but Sheela's were on him.

"Why?" Felix asked, irritated.

"We don't know," Sheela said softly. "If he'd wanted to hurt me, he could have. And that grenade, dear God, you have no idea how terrifying that was. I couldn't hear, couldn't think, couldn't see. But for Lymon pushing me down, I hate to think what it would have been like."

Lymon spread his hands. "Paul heard the flash-bang go off at the same time the guy burst out the door. Our attacker ran all of twenty yards, dove into a cab, and was gone. Vanished."

Rex was still giving him the predatory eye. "Sheela is one of the hottest talents in film today, Lymon. She's worth thirty million a picture. Not to mention that she's a nice person. *Our* person. And you let someone get that close to her? What if that had been a real hand grenade?"

"We'd be dead," Lymon replied reasonably. "But he wasn't trying to kill her."

"But he *could* have!" Felix thundered. "For God's sake, man, that's why we pay you!"

"Enough!" Sheela cried, her blue eyes hardening. "I was *there*. I'm satisfied. I've been with Lymon ever since the event. He's done his job."

Rex, as always, was the first to back down. "Yeah, well, we're scared, that's all." He looked at the newspaper. "It could have been a lot worse than just a couple of canceled shows. And there's the upside. Facebook, Snap Chat, Tik Tok are going bananas. The phones have been ringing off the hooks. Everybody under the sun wants an interview. GMA wants first crack at you. Said they'd bump whomever to get you."

"Screw 'em!" Dot cried. "Last time, they dumped Sheela for Jennifer Lawrence. Paybacks are a bitch."

Felix continued to study Lymon. "You're sure the syringe was empty?"

Lymon shrugged. "I'm not sure of anything. I'm not even sure it was a syringe. It didn't look quite right. In the police report I told them it was 'syringelike.' When he jammed the stun gun into my ribs and I didn't go down, I think he got spooked. I had on enough layers that he didn't get a good connection on the electrodes. Sheela was behind me, supporting me so that I didn't fall. Then there was Dot—she was screaming her head off. I think the guy figured the attack was blown, so he dropped the flash-bang and ran."

"For God's sake, why?" Felix repeated the question that had been tormenting Lymon for two days.

Dot looked from one to the next. "Maybe he's sitting in some bar at Lex and Twenty-Fifth saying, 'Hey, wow! I just scared the shit out of Sheela Marks, man.'"

Felix cocked his head. "I don't get it."

"Neither do I." Lymon answered with a shrug. "It was just a glimpse, but like I say, the syringe looked empty."

"What does that mean?" Rex narrowed one eye into a threatening squint. "What good is an empty syringe?"

"I don't know." Lymon looked up as Tomaso stepped into the room bearing a tray. He placed a glass of sparkling water in front of Sheela and set a cup of coffee to Lymon's right. It was black, just the way he liked it.

"So, what do we do?" Tony leaned forward, a sharpening in his eyes. *"Jagged Cat* is in preproduction.

Costuming wants Sheela in for fitting on Tuesday. Shooting starts on the first."

"So what?" Rex asked. "Sheela's there. What's the big deal? This is our turf." He glanced meaningfully at Lymon. "We can handle it, right?"

Lymon nodded.

Sheela had continued to stare absently at the table in front of her, the sparkling water fizzing by her hand. "It changes your life."

"What's that?" Felix asked.

"Knowing that someone can get that close to you."

"It won't happen again," Rex started, but Sheela raised a hand, cutting him off.

She looked at Lymon. "You've always told me that security wasn't a positive thing. That you could only lessen the odds."

Lymon nodded. "Just as with any system, there's always a way to beat it. Doing it, however, generally takes skill, money, power, luck, or some combination of them."

Sheela studied him thoughtfully. "Which of those do you think was responsible for what happened in New York?"

Lymon sipped his coffee, considering. "Luck is out. My guess is that we're looking at skill and money."

"Why?" Rex demanded.

"It was well planned, which means the guy wasn't counting on luck. The Bureau of Alcohol, Tobacco, Firearms and Explosives controls the sale of flash-bangs to military and police only. This guy had a CTS 7290. He didn't buy it on the corner of Twenty-Second and Park Avenue. It took money to get that uniform. He didn't just lift it out of some guy's locker at the hotel.

So, where'd he get it? Bribe someone in the laundry? Was it even real? Or did some tailor in Midtown make it based on photos of the real thing? Where did he get the key to the storeroom? The hotel ran inventory. None of their five keys for that room are unaccounted for. So, how did the guy know which key opened that door?"

"You're sure he didn't pick the lock?" Felix asked.

Lymon shook his head. "I watched him on the tape, Felix. You could see him reach down, insert it, and turn. It had to be a key. And the guy was cool. He didn't even look up at the camera. He knew he was being recorded, and not once did we get a full facial shot. During the attack his back is toward the camera. Afterward, he runs with his head down and tilted, sort of like a charging bull. Like I said: a pro."

"Rex added, "Thank God Sheela's safe."

"I want to know why," Sheela looked straight at Lymon. "Can you find out?"

Lymon carefully replaced his coffee cup. "Honestly, Sheela, I can try, but I can't promise anything."

"You have connections, don't you?"

"Yeah, sure. But those things cost—"

"I don't care." She used her screen presence, that commanding alto that had carried her to top billing on the marquis. *"Find out!"*

# CHAPTER 4

Sid Harness loosened his tie as he followed the hostess to a table in the back. He liked the Old Ebbitt Grill. The place had atmosphere. He glanced at the brown marble columns on the back bar with their golden chapiters. The stuffed African game heads glared down with fierce glass eyes. Dark wood trim accented the white panels, and the frosted glass dividers seemed to glow with an internal light. The effect was accented by real gas lamps that illuminated historical paintings of the Republic.

From old habit, he took inventory of the occupants: several prominent Washington reporters, one of the congressmen from Ohio with several of his staff members, a basketball star with not one but two fawning blondes at his table. The usual eclectic Washington bunch.

The waitress led Sid to a booth on the back wall, a semi-private affair done in red leather with high seats.

He slid onto the cushions across from Christal Anaya, took the menu, and smiled his thanks as the hostess retreated.

"Sorry I'm late."

Christal arched a thin eyebrow as she studied him from across the table. "If this had been anyplace but the Old Ebbitt Grill, I'd have left a long time ago."

"Development on a case," Sid muttered and preempted the young man who came to ask if he'd like anything to drink. "A Foggy Bottom ale, please."

Sid looked a question at Christal.

She placed a hand over the melted ice in her glass. "I've had enough for now."

After the young man left, Sid cocked his head, watching Christal watch him. God, she was striking. Her midnight black hair gleamed in the fancy gaslights, contrasting with the polished brass above the leather seats. She had a straight nose, sculpted cheeks, and perfect mouth; the sort that demanded a passionate kiss. Spirit lurked within her liquid dark eyes.

"If you're thinking of trying your luck"—her voice was husky with threat—"don't. I'm not big on men right now."

Sid shook his head, sighed, and leaned back, stretching out his arm. "No way, Chris."

The faintest trace of a smile ghosted around her full lips. "Then why would you bring me here?" She indicated the plush restaurant. "It's fancy and expensive, Sid. What's your game?" She narrowed an eye. "Your wife know you're here? With me?"

"Uh-huh."

"Really?" Christal leaned forward, dark locks

spilling over her shoulders. "And just what does she know about me?"

"Everything."

A dark deviltry danced in her eyes. "Everything?"

"Yep. I told Claire I was going out to dinner with a beautiful femme fatale who'd been busted across the chops for something that might have been a simple mistake under other circumstances."

Christal leaned back then, suspicion in her eyes. "So, what's the gig?"

As the waiter stepped up, book in hand, Sid said, "I'd like the New York cut, medium well, baked potato, and ranch dressing."

"The buffalo tenderloin special." Christal shot Sid a sly glance to see if he would recoil at the price. "Medium rare with garlic mashed and a Caesar salad with lots of anchovy."

The waiter stepped away, and she made a chastising gesture with one slim hand. "Normally, in a place like this, the woman is supposed to order first, you know?"

Sid yawned, scratched under his chin, and said, "Yeah. So, I'm a barbarian." He paused. "How you been?"

"Give me a break. How do you think I've been? I feel like hammered shit. When I finally get to sleep, I dream that last meeting in the director's office. I see that son of a bitch sitting there staring at his hands like he was a boy caught shoplifting." She shook her hair back. "I feel like I've been trashed, Sid. I feel like... Hell, I don't know what I feel like. Sick, I guess. Sick in the guts."

"Humiliated?"

"Humiliated." She rolled the drink glass with its

ice back and forth. He watched her thin fingers, the bones so delicate under tanned skin. Her nails looked perfect. "I was headed for a really super career, you know."

At the tone in her voice, he added, "Yeah. Well, it doesn't seem like it, but the resignation was the right thing."

He figured she would have given a sewer rat that same loathing look. "Really?"

"Yeah, they'd have spitted you and roasted you alive. You might feel like shit this way, but you'd have felt like sour vomit the other."

"God, I'm glad you asked me to dinner! I feel so much better now."

"Good." He flipped a card out on the table. "I hear you're thinking about leaving DC. Going back west."

She picked up the card, glancing at it. "You can't be serious?"

"Yep."

"Cut the cowboy crap. Texans and Mexicans have a very long and not-so-nice history, remember?"

"You're from New Mexico."

"Yeah, well Texans and New Mexicans have a long-standing thing between them, too."

"I know. If God had meant for New Mexicans to ski, he would have given them money." Sid grinned. "I know all the old jokes."

He paused, studying her. "About that card, I know the guy. He's always looking for good people. You're one of the best."

"Executive security?" she asked, slightly baffled. "Me? Like a bodyguard?"

Sid nodded.

"Forget it! The first time some skinny rich Anglo mouthed off, I'd bust the teeth out of his head."

"You'd probably be making twice what you are now."

"Was."

"Huh?"

"Twice what I *was* making."

"Oh, right." He proceeded cautiously. "So, what's your plan? Go back to Albuquerque to set up a legal practice? Christal Ayana, attorney at law? Maybe handle some divorces? Draw up estate plans?"

"Hey, I got the degree. A little study and I can re-up on the bar." Her lips twitched. "Even in New Mexico."

Sid grinned at her, reading her defensive smile. "I know. So, you graduated law school third in your class. And what? You slap an application on the FBI's desk first chance you get. You breeze through the qualification and zap, next thing, you're at Quantico; then you're graduated, and sworn in with rave reviews." He cocked his head. "You could have waltzed into a fancy law firm with a starting salary somewhere past a hundred grand. But you took the Bureau. Why?"

Christal studied the card between her fingers. "Do you know what's in all those law books that you see in a lawyer's office, Sid?"

"Cases, right?"

"Law," she answered. "Lawyers, at least good lawyers, spend most of their lives buried in those books. Applying their client's situations to those cases, working up alternatives based on legal decisions."

"Sure."

"I did the books all the way through law school." She glanced up. "And you know what?"

"What?"

For the first time, she actually smiled. "I *hated* it!"

She laughed out loud. "Oh, I was good at it, because that's what I had to be. Hour after hour, I sat and read and memorized. I could quote so-and-so versus what's-his-name and The People versus Whozits. But to do it for the rest of my life?" She made a face.

"Do me a favor?" Sid asked.

The waiter appeared and set Christal's salad in front of her.

"What?"

"Just call the guy. I think he could provide you with enough excitement to keep you from gagging."

As the waiter departed, she poked at her Caesar with a fork, turning one of the brown anchovies over and over. "You're not trying to set me up or anything, are you?"

"Nope."

"Where do you know this guy from?"

"We were both Marine recon. Kosovo, Persian Gulf, Iraq, Afghanistan. He went private while I stayed on the government's payroll. I think you'd like him. He's a no-bullshit kind of guy. Not only that, unlike some of the people in that room the other day, he works in the real world."

She was staring thoughtfully at the card, chewing. He could see her mind working. She asked, "Every job has its downside. What gives here?"

"Boredom. Fatigue." Sid shrugged. "Nothing you're not used to in the field. Hours of sitting on your butt, staying alert, followed by moments of frenetic action. Sometimes horrible hours, sometimes travel. Not that different than investigation, actually."

"He'll ask why I left the Bureau." He could see the air going out of her. "He'll want references, to speak to my supervisor."

Sid speared a bit of carrot. "Nope. He won't need to call anybody."

"What kind of guy is this? He'd just hire someone for a job like this without references?"

"Never."

"But you just said—"

"I've already called him about you. He knows the score, Chris. Like I said, he's been in the shit. He could give a good goddamn what the AD or SAC have to say. I vouched for you."

Her eyes glistened, tears held back by force of will. "Why, Sid?"

He gave her a crooked grin. "Because you're too good to waste. Besides, who knows? Maybe someday you can save my ass."

# CHAPTER 5

Reading traffic was an art. Lymon checked in both directions, made eye contact with the guy in the Chevy truck, and eased the clutch out as he made a right onto Wilshire Boulevard. Traffic was still light. The time 6:38 displayed on the fairing-mounted clock as Lymon tapped his BMW into fourth.

The light changed to yellow and Lymon slowed, downshifting before putting his right foot down. The 1150 RT puttered happily, sending soft vibrations through the seat and bodywork. A motorcycle could be a godsend when it came to Los Angeles traffic. The Japanese crotch rockets might have been faster, but the ass-in-the-air seating position was excruciating. What was the point of looking racy if the position reminded you of a bug snuffling under a cow flop?

When the light turned, Lymon motored past familiar businesses and took a right for a half block to the alley. Turning in, he passed the Dumpsters and waved at the two homeless guys, Stewart and John, who lived under a blue polytarp behind the bakery.

They weren't bad for homeless. They peed and crapped in the storm drain, kept their lash-up neat, and even did odd jobs for the street-front businesses.

Lymon idled into his small parking lot and killed the engine. Pulling off his gloves, he locked them in the tank-side compartment, flipped out the sidestand, and locked the forks.

He pulled his helmet off as he climbed the steel steps to his second-floor offices. After unlocking the door he disarmed the security system and let himself into the back hallway.

He passed the small storeroom to his right, and then walked past the line of cubbyhole offices where his associates held court when they weren't on the job.

Lymon's empire consisted of twelve hundred square feet of the second floor. The rent wasn't bad, considering the location on Wilshire. He was minutes from Beverly Hills, Brentwood, and Pacific Palisades, where most of his clients lived. The second floor wasn't a deterrent to his business. He didn't need a high-traffic location, and most of his clients sent representatives, if they came at all.

Lymon stopped in the cubbyhole where the Capresso machine sat, pushed the button, and watched the lights glow to life. A faint wisp of steam rose from the grate on top. After retrieving his cup from his desk, he filled it, and had just settled in to go through the mail in the inbox when a knock came at the back door.

He frowned at the clock—still ten to seven—and walked back. To his surprise, Mark Ensley stood on the narrow landing. Ensley, too, was in the executive protection business, handling celebrity clients.

Lymon opened the thick security door. "You're

about the last person I expected to find hanging out at my back door. Let me guess, you decided to give up on that two-by-twice outfit you run and come looking for a real job."

"Work for a chickenshit like you? Not a chance in hell. I'd rather hire on as watchman at a junkyard." Ensley stood five-ten and appeared to be in his midthirties when in reality, he was a fit and well-preserved forty-two. He wore an expensive silk sports jacket over a powder blue button-down shirt. Lymon supposed that the bundle in the right-hand coat pocket was the missing tie. Ensley jerked a nod as he stepped into the hallway. His dark eyes looked tired, and his hair was slightly mussed.

"That coffee I smell?" He had a smooth baritone.

"Yeah, and it looks like you need it." Lymon led the way. "Long night?"

"Yeah, weird." Ensley was rubbing the back of his neck. "I was headed home. Took a chance that you might be in early."

"Hey! Glad to be of service. Anything for the competition." Lymon pulled a cup from the rack. "Strong?"

"Yeah. I need all the horsepower I can get."

While the machine ground, steamed, pressed, and dribbled, Lymon cataloged the stress reflected in Ensley's face. Handing him the cup, he led him to the conference room and snaked out a chair before dropping into it backward so he could rest his arms on the back.

The room was paneled in oak veneer with bulletin boards, chalkboards, a screen for PowerPoint and slide projections, as, well as a footlocker full of toys. Actually they were props, used by Lymon's people for planning purposes. With the assortment of blocks, cardboard, and toy cars, they could create most any kind of scale model for route or location briefings.

Ensley flopped into one of the cushioned chairs and stared into his coffee. "What happened in New York? What's your side of the story?"

Lymon detailed it yet again.

When he had finished, Ensley looked up quizzically. "He tried to poke her with a needle? No shit? Like, to inject her with what? HIV? His sperm?"

"You got me."

Ensley sipped at his coffee and raised an eyebrow. Lymon could see faint freckles on his skin. "Hey, that's good. If you keep losing clients, you can go head-to-head with Starbucks."

"I didn't lose my client," Lymon groused, irritated. "But the guy came awfully close."

He met Ensley's eyes. "I can't swear to it—I just got the briefest glimpse—but it looked like the plunger was down on the syringe. Flipped out as it sounds, it was like he was going to try to suck something out of her, not shoot it in. When he finally figured out that the attack was blown, he dropped a flash-bang and ran."

"Huh?" Ensley was skeptical.

"Standard CTS 7290. You might say he was fully committed to escape."

"Maybe it was drugs? Some wacko wanting to share his favorite high with his favorite actress?"

"Or maybe he wanted to inject her with something contagious, something only he had the antidote for? I don't know. Like I said, it looked to me like the plunger was down. Things were happening fast." Lymon settled his chin on his forearms. "So, what brings you to my door? Sure you're not looking for a job? I'll start you at five-fifty an hour taking out the trash."

Ensley grinned but lost it too fast. "Talia had a break-in last night." Talia was Talia Roberts, Sheela's competition for highest-paid top-grossing female star and American icon. "Weird thing. Doesn't make any sense. It was a professional job."

"Talia Roberts has some of the best technology in the business. Sheela's thinking about upgrading to her system."

"Yeah, well, what if I told you some guy parachuted onto her roof last night? He left his chute dangling off the satellite dish just so we'd know for sure. He also left the pitonlike things he screwed into the roof under the tiles and the rope and harness he used to drop over the edge. He cut the screen out of an open third-floor window, and he was in."

"Where's Talia?"

"She had just left the house. She's got a six-a.m. screen call and has to be out for costuming and make-up." Ensley turned the coffee cup in his hands. "The thing is, the guy must know this. You got me as to how. Maybe they were watching from the chopper. When her car pulled out of the drive, the guy dropped out the hatch."

"So...what did he take?"

Ensley looked up. "That's the weird thing. He took her sheets. Right off the bed. Still, like warm, you know? That, and the trash out of the bedroom waste-basket. What kind of guy steals dirty sheets and bedroom trash?"

"I'd start watching eBay. Maybe Talia's trash sells for a whole lot."

Ensley didn't look amused. "So, the guy bags up the sheets and trash, then climbs out the window. Up to now it's been a perfect job. Julia's people find out she's been hit because the helicopter comes in low, drops a line, and snags the guy off the roof. Woke up half the neighborhood."

Lymon rubbed his chin. "Like he didn't care if anyone found out that he'd been there?"

"Yeah. The police have already been in touch with the FAA. Did you know there were a hundred and thirty-seven helicopters flying in the LA Basin? Traffic control actually had the chopper on their screens for a while until they lost it against the San Gabriels." Ensley made a waving gesture. "Do you know how many private heliports there are up in those multimillion-dollar estates? He could have gone anywhere."

"I'd start checking with the rental companies. Not just everyone has a copter for hire. What about the house? The thief leave anything?"

Ensley sipped his coffee. "Police just finished going over Talia's room with a microscope. Nothing. *Nada*. Not a print, nor hair, nor bit of fabric. Nothing on the ropes, pitons, or parasail. It's all clean. You'd think it was the CIA or something."

"How's Talia?"

"Freaked." He looked up, grinning weakly. "You may be up to your neck in job apps when she gives me the boot."

"Once she settles down, she won't fire you, Mark. You couldn't have known some creep was going to parachute in, for God's sake." Lymon cocked his head. "It was too well planned. Not just some obsessive fan." He paused. "Shit."

"What?"

"I don't know. Just shit. Who'd want dirty sheets? I mean, why not take something really personal, like her Oscar, or jewelry, or a dress, or something?"

"I'm stumped, Lymon." He tossed off the last of his coffee. "I just needed to talk it over." He glanced at his watch. "For now, I'm headed home for a nap. Talia's got a meeting with her people at three this afternoon. This shit's gonna be all over the tube tonight, and I'd better be sharp enough to stick in the floor when it happens."

"Yeah." Lymon stood. "Listen, if there's anything we can do for you?"

Ensley grinned. "Nah. But if she cans me, I'll put in a good word for you. She's got to go somewhere."

# CHAPTER 6

The waiting was driving Christal mad. She had packed most of her small Alexandria apartment. The boxes sat in neat stacks in her living room. On the TV, the talking heads on Capitol News were reviewing the sports world. For something to do, she'd taken up pacing both the length and breadth of her small apartment. She'd liked it here, had considered it home while she built a nest egg bank account in preparation for down payment on a real house one day.

Christal paused by the breakfast bar to stare at the phone. She tapped her fingernails on the countertop and sighed. Lifting the receiver, she punched the familiar numbers.

*"Harness,"* the voice on the end said.

"Hey, Sid."

*"Christal? What's up?"*

"What are you doing?"

*"Kidnapping. Young woman. Graduate student at Washington. Real hotshot. Some kind of genetics research. Hey, did you know there's a string of unsolved kidnappings of geneticists going back five years?"*

"No, Sid. I didn't know that." She glanced at the TV. "Most of the news is about Taylor Swift. Someone ripped off her penthouse in New York. Took her hairbrush. Can you imagine?"

*"You haven't called Lymon yet."*

"I've been packing."

*"Where you going?"*

"I don't know."

*"Call Lymon. Me, I've got three more interviews to conduct. You wouldn't believe some of the things they can do with genetics these days."* He chuckled. *"In theory, at least."*

"Sounds like fun." She hesitated. "Wish I was there." She meant it.

Sid heard the undertones. *"Call Lymon. I mean it. Meanwhile, I've got to figure out if my missing person is related to the sixteen priors."*

"Sixteen?" she asked, amazed. "God, why haven't we heard about this?"

*"We're just putting it together. Call Lymon. I gotta go."*

She heard the line go dead. Glancing at the television, she saw the camera was giving a shot of the street in front of the singer's ritzy building in New York.

# CHAPTER 7

Lymon really appreciated Sheela Marks' pool. It was huge—like everything else in the house —but when an A-list star like Sheela made thirty million a picture plus residuals, she could have a lot of perks.

The pool might have been a bit short of Olympic size, but the fitted-stone patio with its ivy-shaded trelliswork and overhanging live oak made for a cool and delightful sanctuary. A full-size Richard Greeves bronze of Sacagawea stood to the right, her face lifted to the sunlight. The few muted sounds of civilization—traffic and airplanes, mostly—that managed to seep past the high wall were drowned by the bubbling fountains that dominated the flower beds to either side.

Lymon stepped out of the double French doors after checking to make sure the wires to the security sensors were still attached and unfrayed. Old habits and all that.

Sheela sat in a lounge chair, a script in her hand.

Lymon identified it by the brass brads in the three binding holes. She was in Balenciaga jeans and wearing a William B white cotton blouse unbuttoned over a turquoise tube top. Her red-blond hair had been done in a French braid. A glass of what looked like iced lemonade stood on the marble table beside her.

Lymon seated himself on the padded wrought-iron chair across from her and waited. Even after three years of association, she still affected him. Tall and long-legged, she carried herself with a sense of grace that no one would have associated with her obscure Canadian origins.

"Where do they get this shit?" she asked, smacking the pages she held. She looked up and fixed him with her irritated blue eyes.

"Got me. I don't write the things."

She shook her head and tossed the script onto the cement beside her. "I read it before it went into development. Good stuff, nice idea. Now, the execs have been having meetings. It's been through two rewrites by four people, and it's shit! I'm on page thirty, and I already know that by the third act my character is going to be raped by her father. So now I'm shooting him in the last scene? Duh!"

"Yeah, well, you shouldn't complain. I know for a fact that producers and studio execs don't get put in charge of really hot properties until their lobotomies have fully healed."

She grinned at that.

"What did you want to see me about?" Lymon rubbed his hands together. "Are my people on the ball?"

She lifted an eyebrow. "You come on your bike?"

Lymon nodded.

Sheela stood. "Come on." She led the way back into the house, calling to Tomaso as she passed, "Lymon and I are going out for a while. If Rex calls, he can get me on my cell."

"Yes, ma'am."

Lymon lifted a brow as they stopped by the front door. Sheela stepped into the coatroom and returned wearing a white leather jacket and carrying a pearlescent helmet.

"Sheela, just what the hell do you think you're doing?"

"We're going for a ride. You and me."

"Are you nuts?"

"Are you armed?" She pointed at his armpit, where he kept his HK .40 Compact in a Kramer undervest. "Of course you are. So, I'm well-guarded and safe, right? Come on, Lymon. We need to talk. Just you and me." She rolled her eyes to indicate the opulent surroundings. "Away from here."

Her smile would have melted Kevlar. "And it's been years since I've been on a bike."

"What if something-—"

"It's an *order*, Lymon. If I can't trust you, who the hell can I?"

"It's not a matter of trust. It's about variables that I can't control: drunk drivers, spilled oil on the road, an errant SUV with underinflated tires, and a malfunctioning guidance system."

"Is that a harried housewife?"

"Generally."

"We're going."

With misgivings bubbling in his breast, he led the way out to the silver BMW. "In my professional opinion, I have to inform you that I think this is a bad idea. My job—"

"Is to keep your client happy," she shot back. "Aren't you the one who lives by the mantra 'The principal comes first'? Damn, I should have had Felix draw up a release, but that would have led to too many questions."

He stopped, taking his helmet off the handlebar. "We could have Paul bring the limo around. Anything you have—"

*"Don't you get it?"* Her eyes were pleading. "I'm tired of living in a can, Lymon. And you're the head canner!"

He helped her with her helmet, surprised that it was not only the right size, but DOT and Snell approved. "You've been planning this?"

"Ever since we got back from New York."

He straddled the bike, steadying it as she climbed on. "You've ridden before?"

"When I was a kid. Dad had a Harley and an old 250 Yamaha for farm work."

"Just do what I do. If we go down, hang on to me." He thumbed the starter, and the Beemer lit. Toeing it into gear, he let the clutch out and eased around the circle. At the gate, they waited while the heavy iron rolled back.

"I'll bet John's wondering who the second rider is."

She laughed. "Yeah, it's good for him."

"Where to?"

"Up to the Ventura, east to Glendale, and then take

Highway Two over the Angeles Crest. After that, we'll make it up as we go."

She *had* planned it.

Lymon wound around, caught Beverly Glenn north to the Ventura Freeway, and matched speed with the traffic.

"Wahoo!" Sheela cried on the back as she raised her arms to the wind. "I am *free*!"

*She's free, and I feel like I'm carrying a case of nitroglycerine in the tour pack!*

He didn't know how long it had been since he felt so nervous. Damn it! What if he dropped it with Sheela Marks on board? The woman sitting behind him was worth somewhere in the neighborhood of a billion dollars by the time you figured in future box office, residuals, and advertising revenue. The lawsuits would take years. This was lunacy!

"Doesn't this thing go any faster than fifty-five?" she called over his shoulder.

"I was just trying to calculate your net worth if I killed you."

"According to the latest figures Rex put together, about one point two billion. Now, take a deep breath, and let's move with the rest of the traffic."

He made a face, signaled, and felt the BMW surge as he accelerated into the fast lanes.

They made it to the twisty two-lane outside of La Canada Flintridge, and Lymon eased into the first of the corners.

"Doesn't this thing lean?" Sheela asked over his shoulder as she wrapped her arms around his waist. "You've got tread all the way up the sides of the tires. I saw it back at the house."

"Most strung-out actresses use pills," he muttered.

"What? Pills?"

"Yeah, you know, for committing suicide." With that, he figured himself for dead anyway, twisted the wick, and let the big twin do its thing.

# CHAPTER 8

ANGELES CREST

How long had it been since she felt this relaxed? Sheela tilted her head back and looked up through the branches spreading above her. It was a pine tree. Even she knew that much. The can of Dr Pepper felt delightfully cool in her hands. A crystal creek was bubbling just to her left as she sat on a lichen-covered rock with her feet on a brown bed of needles.

"Perfect," she purred to herself. She could feel knots loosening in her muscles. For this one blissful moment, the world was fading, the pressure lessening.

She glanced at Lymon. He was standing to one side, looking antsy as he gazed back up the hill at the little gas station and store where they had pulled off the road. The sleek silver BMW was just visible at the edge of the parking lot.

"Relax, Lymon. Take yourself off the payroll for a minute."

He smiled at her, the action wary. "Can't, Sheela. It's just who I am. You've already talked me into a potential major-league fuckup."

She looked around at the trees and listened to the wind sighing in the branches. A loud car blasted past on the highway above them, exhaust howling. "So, how do you assess the risk here? High? We're on the edge of the forest. It's the wrong part of the country for *Deliverance,* and you don't look anything like Burt Reynolds."

"I guess I don't at that."

She studied him, trying to read his hard face. He had been a mystery since the first time she'd met him. Her previous security personnel had been pretty straightforward. They had cop personalities: That easy swagger, inside sense of kindred, and cynical approach to life she had known since her days as a teenager in Regina.

"You were a soldier," she remarked. "Special forces?"

"Recon. Same thing, but different." He looked at her. "Why are we doing this?"

She reached down for a pine cone and studied the brittle triangular petals. "I had to get away. I want to talk to you." That made him even more nervous.

She decided to let him off the hook. "Lymon, I want you to look into something for me."

He lifted a craggy eyebrow, waiting.

"This thing that happened in New York, it's been bothering me."

"Look, Sheela, we're instituting new procedures for the next time we're on the road."

She waved him down. "It's not that. I grew up in the real world. I know you can't stop everyone one hundred percent of the time. At least not and still let me do my job. I've got to go places, make appearances, and play the game."

"Okay, so?"

"So, I want you to figure out what this is all about."

"What have you heard?"

"Talia's bedsheets. Someone just stole a lock of John Lennon's hair from a museum. My attack, all high profile, all perfectly planned. Something you said at the meeting stuck with me: skill, power, money, and luck. Those were the things you said someone needed to beat a system. If we throw out luck, that leaves skill, power, and money."

"Uh-huh. So?"

"It doesn't make sense. Anyone with money and power who wanted to touch me, could. He could wrangle an invitation to a party or put leverage on Tony or Rex. He could buy his way onto the set for *Jagged Cat,* or glad-hand his way into a fundraiser or release party."

"I suppose."

"It wouldn't cost more than renting a helicopter, say, or figuring out how to break Taylor Swift's security system. I am assuming that those things can be had, but for a pretty hefty price."

He was watching her warily. "That's right."

"Lymon, part of my job is hype. I'm a product, marketed and sold. I know I have a certain charisma that translates on-screen. The rest of it is how I'm pack-aged. Hell, even a lot of the crap in social media is manipulated by Dot and Rex."

"What are you trying to get at?"

"Marketing."

"I'm not sure I follow you."

"I'm not sure I follow me either. It's just a hunch." She tossed the pine cone to one side. "But it feels right."

He nodded, frowning. "Okay, so, marketing what? Weaknesses in security?"

"That's what I want you to find out." She stood, drinking down the last of her soda. "Now, while you think about it, let's go ride. I want to enjoy every second before they put me back in the can."

# CHAPTER 9

The air-conditioning was humming its familiar chant as Lymon sat at his desk. He kept running his day with Sheela over and over in his head when he was supposed to be concentrating on paperwork. Through the open door he could hear June Rosen, the secretary, talking on the phone out front. From her tone of voice—excruciatingly polite —he knew it wasn't good.

Neither was his current task. He hated accounting and thanked God every day that June could do most of it. She wrote the checks for the electricity, water, rent, insurance, and the rest. She calculated the 941 payment, made sure that W-2s were up-to-date. She kept track of employee hours and tallied the expense report receipts, then calculated and sent the billing. The burden of double-checking schedules and making travel arrangements fell onto her shoulders, and like now, she answered the phone.

Lymon heard it click; then came the sound of June's pumps as she walked back and leaned in the door. She was a wholesome-looking thirty-two, two kids, single after a second divorce. Today she had her brown-blond hair up in something Lymon would have called a beehive. She wore a charcoal cotton pullover.

"That was *Daily Variety* again. They're still prying away at the New York incident. They are wondering if it could be related to Talia's break-in."

Lymon tapped the expense reports with his pen. "Maybe Sandra Bullock and Gal Gadot will get hit next? Someone who grosses big like Sheela?"

He paused at that, remembering Sheela's insistence that it was all tied somehow to marketing.

"You okay?" June asked. "You've been preoccupied all day."

"Yeah, fine. Thanks." He smiled as she ducked back and clumped her way to the front desk.

Truth was, he'd been off his feed ever since that crazy ride with Sheela. After their soda stop, she'd insisted that they ride clear over to Santa Clarita before heading back. He had deposited her at her door a little before nine that night.

That look she had given him when she said "Thank you" had left him even more unsettled. Her eyes had been shining, intense—and they had looked straight into his soul.

*Knock it off! She's business.*

Security personnel didn't get involved with their principals. Not only was it morally irresponsible, it was downright dangerous. He was in enough trouble over the New York disaster.

His mind kept returning to that spirited ride. He'd been prudent, hadn't pushed the envelope, but once he'd relaxed, forgotten who was on the back, it had been fabulous.

The phone jangled at his elbow. He picked it up, hearing June: *"Sid Harness for you on line one."*

Lymon punched the button and said, "Sid? What's up?"

*"Did Christal ever call you?"*

"Nope."

*"Oh, hell."*

"Look, maybe she doesn't want the job."

*"She's her own worst critic. Still blaming herself. I don't know. It's just that she's too good to lose. You know what I mean? She's young, and this is the first time she's really taken a hit. And it was a bad one. She's one of the best. Got a nose for what's really happening, you know? It's like she can sniff out motive. Hell, she was the one who broke the Gonzales case before it got FUBARed."*

Lymon considered that. Motive? That was what was bothering him, Ensley, and Sheela. He tapped his pen on the reports. His people were trained to be guard dogs, not wolves.

*"Lymon? You still there?"*

"Sid? Maybe she's not right for executive protection. It's an art, a calling if you will, rather than a nine-to-five job. It takes a certain kind of personality. You know, someone who can whip a Escalade through a J-turn one minute and walk the principal's dog the next. This Anaya, she's a street agent, right? Trained to stick her nose into trouble, not cover and evacuate a principal."

*"She's got the brains for it, Lymon. Isn't that what you've always told me? That the job was really thinking out of the box? Planning? Advance study of a location or event?"*

"Yeah, so? If she was that smart, how'd she get her tit in a wringer over this Gonzales thing?"

*"What would have happened if someone had recorded your, um,* indiscretion *with that sultan's daughter?"*

"I'd have been court-martialed on the spot and still sitting in jail in Djibouti today." Lymon winced. "Hey, I was young. I've never fucked up since."

An image of Sheela stared at him with cerulean eyes, and his heart skipped. Crap! He couldn't do it again. Wouldn't.

*"Christal's young, too. Unlike you, she got busted. So tell me, you've been there. Second chances can make all the difference, can't they? Or have you stopped believing in learning from your mistakes?"*

Sheela's words haunted him: *Lymon, I want you to figure out what this is all about.*

He took a deep breath. "Sid, if I wanted her to do a little digging for me, maybe stuff that was OTR, off the record, could she do it?"

*"In spades, buddy. I swear, she's as good as they come."*

"What is she to you?"

There was a long pause. Finally, Sid said, *"Yeah, okay, maybe I'm a little bit in love with her. Just trust me on this, all right? When have I ever steered you wrong?"*

"What about time you thought it would be a good idea to smear Vaseline on the colonel's—"

*"That doesn't count. I don't jack around when lives are at stake."*

"Give me her number, Sid."

# CHAPTER 10

The tape made a ripping sound as Christal stripped it from the roll and sealed the last box. Using her teeth, she bit it off and patted it snug on the brown cardboard. Her apartment was cleaned, all traces of her gone but for the stack of brown boxes, each carefully labeled. The moving guys would be coming within the hour to load them into the van. Three days later, they would unload them at her mother's house in Nambe, New Mexico. Whenever Christal was ready for them, they'd be stacked in Mom's garage.

Her remaining personal possessions consisted of a pile of clothing to be hung in the back of her old battered 2015 Nissan, her suitcase, two plants, and the radio that was playing on the breakfast bar.

She stood and tossed the roll of tape into her open suitcase. At the mention of Mel Gibson's name on the radio, she stopped short. She'd always liked his work.

*"Sydney police remain baffled as they reconstruct the break-in at Sydney's prestigious Regent Hotel. Gibson certainly isn't in for a close shave in his next film, since it seems the erstwhile thieves only took the shaver head from his electric razor."*

Christal wrinkled her nose and tossed her thick black hair over her shoulder. She remembered the scuzzy stuff that an electric razor collected: bits of skin, chopped fragments of beard. Hell, if she was hitting Mel's place, she'd go for his checkbook, credit cards, and Swiss bank account—assuming he had one.

"Or, how about his agent's phone number while I'm at it, huh?"

She walked into the kitchen, opened the refrigerator door, and found a half-empty carton of orange juice. She set it on the counter before tossing opened jars of mustard, pickles, ketchup, and mayonnaise into the trash. When she lifted the lid on a plastic container in the far back, she found the green fuzzy remains of a month-old casserole. Good riddance. The nearly empty jar of Greek olives she kept, opening the lid and popping one into her mouth. She'd packed her glasses, so she lilted the orange juice carton back and chugged.

The phone rang. Wiping her mouth, she pulled her phone from her back pocket. Didn't recognize the area code. If it was the moving guys telling her they'd be late, she was going to raise hell.

"Hello?"

*"Is this Christal Anaya?"* The voice was male, competent sounding.

"Yeah. Who's this?"

*"Sid Harness gave me your number. My name is Lymon*

Bridges, of Lymon Bridges Associates Personal Security, LLC. My business is—"

"Yeah, I know." She made a face. "Look, I don't know that I'd be any good at babysitting celebrities. You know, it's that bullshit factor."

To his credit, he laughed. *"Yeah, you get that on occasion, but not so much from the kind of people my agency works for. Most of them know the stakes."*

"Well, you see, Mr. Lyman—"

*"Bridges. I'm Lymon Bridges."*

"Mr. Bridges, the point I'd like to make is that I'm not in the market for a job right now."

*"Previous offer? How much are they paying?"*

She gave the phone a deadly smile, figuring, *What the hell?* "I don't think you could touch it."

*"If you're as good as Sid says you are, and if everything works out, I'll start you at ten thousand a month plus expenses."*

Christal stopped short. "Excuse me?"

*"I think you heard—although the slip over my name doesn't lend credence to your investigative abilities."*

"That was meant to irritate you."

*"It worked."* A pause. *"Are you as good as Sid says you are?"*

She shook her head, confused. "I don't know. Ten thousand a month? Just to keep some stuck-up spoiled movie star out of trouble? I don't have the ten-ton-gorilla physique. I'm five-six and weigh one-fifteen."

*"But you broke the Enrique Gonzales case open? Sid says you did that where the rest of the Bureau couldn't."*

*And blew it all!* Aloud, she asked, "Do you pay all of your bodyguards ten thousand?"

"No. Most of them are off-duty cops trying to make their bills. But you're not exactly going to be a part-time agent."

She felt her hackles rising. God, he hadn't seen the photos, had he? She tried to keep the rage out of her voice. "Just what did you have in mind?"

"Did you hear the news today? About Mel Gibson's razor?"

That left her off balance. "Yeah."

"There's an open E-ticket for you at Dulles. Delta counter. I'll have someone meet you at LAX soonest. Just give me a call with your flight number and arrival time."

"Just like that? Fly to Los Angeles?"

"I have some people here I would like you to meet. There are things I want you to look into for us. If you are as good as Sid says, maybe you can do it. Then again, maybe you can't. Which is okay." A pause. "Let me know which flight."

Then the son of a bitch hung up.

Christal stared at the phone, listening to the dial tone. What the hell? Did he think she was just going to drop everything and fly to Los Angeles?

She cocked her head. Mel Gibson's razor? She could feel curiosity twirling around her spine like growing ivy.

"Bullshit! It's all bullshit."

# CHAPTER 11

June arched a critical eyebrow. "You didn't even give her our phone number."

Lymon leaned back in his chair and laced his fingers behind his head. "She's an investigator, isn't she? If she can't find our phone number, what the hell good is she?"

"She's not coming."

"She'll be walking off a jetway by noon tomorrow."

June shook her head. "Twenty bucks says no."

"You're on."

She gave him that suspicious look. "I don't get it. All you've got is Sid's word on this woman. She's just been canned at the FBI, so what makes you think she might be capable of doing this...whatever it is you're doing?"

Lymon shrugged. "One, I know Sid. He knows me, and he knows talent. I know what she did at the FBI, and Sid still vouches for her. That tells me that she might have fucked up, but it's not a genetic predisposition. Two, if she's not walking out of that jetway by noon tomorrow—or on the phone telling me she's delayed for a damn good reason—she's not the right person for the job. For twenty bucks, it's cheap at twice the price."

"I don't want you around my boys," June told him as she started down the hall. "I'm trying to raise them to be decent and normal human beings."

"What? You think I'm like a lawyer or something?"

"More like a politician, actually."

"Hey! There's no reason to get ugly."

# CHAPTER 12

"In preparation for landing, please place your tray tables in their stowed position and return your seats to the upright position. All personal items must be stowed under the seat in front of you or in the overhead bins. At this time, all personal electronic devices must be turned off. Thank you."

Christal found the button that made the footrest retract and brought her seat upright. She folded the table into the seat arm and turned off the reading light that hung by her ear. Once her laptop was zipped into its bag, she used her toe to shove it under the seat in front of her.

She glanced around, handing her used glass to the stewardess who walked past. If Lymon Bridges was trying to impress her, he was definitely on the right track. She'd almost gaped like the village idiot when the ticket agent told her that a first-class ticket was confirmed.

*"Christal, what do you think about the Secret Service?"* Sid had asked when she'd called him from Dulles. *"I mean the guys that oversee the president's safety. The real agents that do the actual work."*

When she'd given him an affirmative answer, he'd said, *"That's Lymon Bridges. That's the kind of work he does. He's one of the best, working for the best. I personally vouch for the guy. Trust me, if you don't think he's square, I'll buy your plane ticket back."*

She wondered if Sid knew he would have to shell out for first class.

Christal leaned her head back. Since seeing her belongings loaded into the moving van for New Mexico, her time had been spent on two subjects. First off, she caught herself wondering if this was such a good idea, and second, she had bought every news magazine in the WHSmith stand at Dulles to read up on celebrities. During the flight, she had used the first-class Internet access to do further research on her laptop.

The results had perplexed her. Mel Gibson's razor, John Lennon's lock of hair, Talia Roberts' sheets, Sheela Marks' odd assault—they all reeked of the bizarre. The thing that really aroused her curiosity as an FBI...okay, an ex-FBI agent, was that each of the crime scenes was clean. No clues had been left. Nothing. That, more than anything, made her whiskers quiver.

So, were they related? If so, how? What was the point? How much value did Talia Roberts' sheets have on the street? Christal made a face. She was definitely a Mel Gibson fan, but she wouldn't give a dented quarter for the chaff in his electric razor. Very well then, if you threw out cash, what was next?

*It's some pervert with big bucks who's intent on sending them some kind of message.*

Then why didn't he call, write a letter, or email? Pranksters liked to taunt in words as well as action.

A prank? Perhaps it was someone in the movie business? Maybe some director or producer—one who had inadvertently misplaced his life somewhere along the way and had nothing better to do than think up weird nonsense like this?

She mulled the notion as the 767 banked on approach. Looking through the window, she could see Los Angeles baking under the morning sun. Brown haze was packed up over San Bernardino and Riverside.

The sheer size of the sprawling megalopolis surprised her. She'd never seen it from the air before. The last time she had been in the city was as a little girl, when Mama had driven to Anaheim to see Aunt Maria. She remembered that trip as an eternity between potty breaks. She'd been hot, stuffed in the back seat with her unruly brothers. Aunt Maria had lived in a crowded apartment building. Christal and her brothers had been bored the entire time, fighting constantly and being yelled at. On top of it all, they hadn't gone to Disneyland.

She winced as the big jet touched down. A curious anticipation built as the plane taxied to its gate. She had that sense that her life was changing. Usually, when she felt this way, it was for a reason. She'd felt it the moment she submitted her application to law school, had felt it again when the FBI sent her a letter of acceptance, and felt it yet again the night she and Hank had made love in the surveillance van—though that had been one hell of a misinterpretation of presentiment.

As the bell rang and the seat belt sign went off, she stood, retrieved her laptop and carry-on from the bin, then filed out.

Christal didn't really expect anyone in the gate area, security being what it was and LAX having been a constant target. To her surprise, she immediately saw the woman with the hand-lettered ANAYA sign. Anyone from a car service should have been on the other side of security.

She walked up, set her carry-on down, and extended her hand. "I'm Christal Anaya."

"June Rosen." The woman's smile had a wry quality, her handshake firm. "Welcome to LA. Do you have any other bags?"

"Just these. I travel light."

"This way then." Rosen reached for the bag, but Christal snatched it up.

"I can carry it."

As they walked, she glanced sidelong at the woman. "I would have expected Mr. Bridges."

"Lymon, damn his hide, is in an advance meeting with Universal. They're ironing out the details for *Jagged Cat.*"

"Excuse me? Why 'damn his hide,' and what's a jagged cat?"

June gave her a crooked grin. "Second question first. *Jagged Cat* is the client's new picture. They're in pre-production right now. That's costuming, building sets, and all the stuff that's got to be done before filming. The studios have pretty good security, but Lymon has to make sure that our people interface with theirs so that we can pick her up and drop her off, have the right passes, and so forth. We need to know the shooting schedule and where, if anywhere, we're going on location."

"Huh?"

"Are they shooting a scene in Portugal? If so, we have to be ready, advance the location, check the hotels, establish a relationship with local law enforcement, make reservations for our people, and book travel."

Christal thought about that. "Doesn't the studio do all that?"

"Sure, but what if Sheela wants to go sightseeing between scenes? Does she have transportation? Do we need local security? Special permits? Are there areas she shouldn't travel through? High-crime zones? What if she gets sick or is injured, maybe has an allergic reaction to something? That's our responsibility."

"I didn't know it was that complicated." She wondered who Sheila was.

"Sometimes more so."

"And the 'damn his hide'?"

"I bet the bastard twenty bucks you wouldn't show."

Christal smiled, deciding she liked June Rosen. "And what do you do for Lymon Bridges?"

"In official terms, I'm the secretary. In blunt actuality, I'm the business manager. I run the company." She shot Christal a communicative glance. "Fortunately for him, he's never asked me to sit on his lap, iron his shirts, or make coffee."

"How long have you been with the company?"

"Three years now."

"Is it a good springboard?"

June led her out through security. "Sure. But why would I go anywhere else? My boys are in good schools, and I get paid to work my ass off. Paid *well*."

Christal considered that as they passed the ticket counters and stepped out into the warm day. A snazzy black Cadillac Escalade sat at the curb, its four-ways flashing. June pressed a button on a key fob, and the lights flashed.

"You can just leave it in the Arrivals lane?"

"Special permit." June stepped to the trunk, opening it so Christal could place her bag inside.

Seating herself in the plush passenger seat, Christal looked around. Giant SUVs had never been her thing. She liked small, compact, and parkable. But then, she'd never had a special permit before.

June started the engine, fastened her seat belt, and waved at a cop who stopped oncoming vehicles to allow them into traffic.

"The special permit gets you into the concourses, too?"

"Only at LAX. Lymon has done a lot of work fostering good relations with the TSA team here." She smiled and tapped her purse. "It helps that I'm a special deputy with LA County."

"Do I get a special permit?"

"You'll have to take that up with Lymon," June said cryptically. Then she turned her attention to driving as she accelerated northbound onto the San Diego Freeway. Christal noted that the woman held the wheel professionally and handled the big car with confident ease.

"First class, special permits, tricked-out Escalades —you people don't exactly keep a low profile, do you?"

"In this town, Ms. Anaya, image is marketing." She glanced at Christal. "How is your wardrobe?"

"I beg your pardon?"

"Depending on the nature of the principal's appearance, you will be required to dress in anything from professional to very formal. The problem with formal is to still look good but have freedom of movement in case things get, shall we say, athletic."

"I don't get it."

"Have you ever seen a Hollywood gala on TV?"

"Sure."

"Could you pick the bodyguards out of the crowd?"

"Well, yeah, sometimes. They're the big guys who look unhappy."

"How about the women?"

"I didn't know there were any."

June smiled dryly. "That's precisely what we're looking for."

# CHAPTER 13

"**I**t's *not* going to happen!" Sheela's voice carried from the dressing room as Lymon walked onto the set where the wardrobe session was in progress. At first glance, he saw Paul over in the corner under a stand of lights. The driver was sitting backward in a chair, a barely concealed grin struggling to creep past his iron control.

According to Lymon's watch, Sheela should be halfway through her fitting session. This was the first time the costume designers actually saw their creations on the stars.

Two assistants huddled to one side, slightly horrified expressions on their faces. Rex stood to the right, arms crossed over his belly and looking dour. Three different photographers were spotted here and there around the room with a plethora of cameras on tripods as well as hanging from straps on their necks.

The fitting room was studded with lights and reflectors focused on a raised dais. Mirrors were positioned so that the star could get a three-hundred-sixty-degree view of herself in costume. In the rear stood rack after rack of hanging dresses, blouses, suits, and jackets.

Lymon stopped short when he caught sight of Sheela standing on the dais.

Her face had that look of absolute disgust that he had grown passingly familiar with over the years. She was wearing a bright red sparkly gown with what he'd call "wings" sprouting off of each shoulder. It fit glove-tight at her slim waist, advertised her rounded breasts, and clung to her thighs.

"It's looov'ly," Fiona Borg cooed, a rapturous look on her wrinkled face. She had her gray hair tucked in a wretched hat—the sort of thing for which she would have paid a fortune to an obscure Italian designer—and wore something that reminded Lymon of a silver sheet wrapped around her bony frame.

"I look like the princess in *Dune* 2!" Sheela countered. "The wings go...and the color can be anything but bright red."

"But vee 'ave already chosen. Bernard loooves it!"

Sheela whirled, her finger like a dagger. "Change it! I could give a shit what Bernard loves. This thing makes me look like the vampire whore in *Blood Guzzler*."

"But I—"

"Do I have to call Felix to read you the clause in the contract? The dress goes, or I do." She reached back and struggled for the clasps in the back.

"The dress is out, Fiona," Rex interjected with authority. "If Bernard's got questions, he can call."

"So, vhat?" Fiona asked, waving her thin arms. "Vee got vhat? Two veeks to shooting, huh? You vant me to conjure from t'in air?"

One of the assistants had sprung up to help Sheela with the clasps and zippers. Lymon could see Sheela's frustration in the tight movements of her arms as she wiggled out of the fabric. In a bra and panties, she stepped free, and then with a toe, kicked the gaudy creation off the stage. She noticed Lymon for the first time, smiled, and rolled her eyes in an indication of frustrated endurance.

For his part, he tried not to stare. Sure, he'd seen her body before, at fittings, when she was in the pool, and during photography. That was before that same body had been pressed so close to his on the bike. Before she'd given him that haunting look.

"We'll figure something out," Rex said, trying to placate Fiona. The woman had won two Oscars for costume design, which placed her in the sacred realm of the Hollywood gods.

"Ya, ya. You try dis, huh?" Fiona thrust a hand at the racks of clothing. "You t'ink dis is easy? Making de dress, makes de scene, ja?"

"We've got some problems with the screenplay as it is," Rex soothed. "Just find something Sheela likes. It's the wings, Fiona. She looks like an overbruised bat in them."

"And the color!" Sheela sang out.

"And the color," Rex agreed. "The set's basically painted what color? Blue or something?"

Sheela held up her hand. "I'll do red. Just not in that contraption." She glanced meaningfully at Lymon. "Give me five, people. I need to talk to Mr. Bridges for a moment. Business."

The assistants and Rex clustered around Fiona, all talking in serious voices as Sheela stepped off the dais, grabbed a white terry cloth robe, and wrapped it around herself before walking over.

"I thought I'd give your eyeballs a break," she said with a smile. "I've never seen you look at me like that."

"Sorry," he muttered, hating himself for feeling slightly embarrassed. "Thought I'd let you know: We're square with the studio. Everything's set. Paul's your guard dog and gofer when you're on the lot. If you need anything special, just ask him. He calls the office, and we're on it. Like always, the more advance notice, the better off we are."

She nodded, looking back at the pile of red fabric with the two wings lying akimbo. "Can you imagine they wanted me to wear that? I'm supposed to shoot my father, for God's sake. Wearing that? What are they thinking of?"

"Tinkerbell goes vamp?"

"Maybe." She turned back toward him. "And the other subject we discussed the other day?"

"June picked someone up at the airport. I'll be meeting with her as soon as everything is thumbs-up here."

"Who?"

"Someone an old friend turned me on to. Ex-FBI. Supposedly smart, talented, and motivated. I won't know until I actually talk to her."

"Her?" Sheela arched an eyebrow. "Isn't that a little unusual?"

"Maybe. Yeah." He shrugged, seeing the hesitant curiosity in her eyes.

"Bring her to the house. I want to meet her."

He frowned, wondered at her probing blue gaze. "Yes, ma'am."

She narrowed a chastening right eye. "And stop the 'yes ma'am' stuff. It makes me nervous."

"Yes, ma'am."

She gave an exasperated sigh, pulling him farther off to the side. "Lymon, you're acting nervous. Was it the motorcycle ride?"

"Yes, ma'am."

"It's really irritating when you say that."

"Yes, ma'am."

Are you afraid that I might try to change our relationship?"

"Yes, ma'am."

"And you don't trust yourself to stay professional?"

"Ms. Marks, people in my profession—"

"Lymon, this isn't the time or place to have this discussion." She looked back to where Rex was still arguing with Fiona. "I've got to go." She reached for his left arm, turning his wrist so she could see the time. "Bring this person to the house. I should be there by three, which means I'll really be there by five."

"Yes, ma'am."

She gave him her million-dollar smile. "We'll talk about you and me some other time. It's not what you're afraid of."

*Isn't it?* The words echoed in his head as she turned and walked back to the knot around Fiona.

# CHAPTER 14

At precisely four that afternoon, Christal walked out of her unit. She appreciated the choice of a Marriott Residence Inn for her lodging. Not only did she have more room than in a hotel, but she had filled out the grocery list and looked forward to cooking her own breakfast. Having grown up in New Mexico, the average American breakfast of eggs, pig meat, potatoes, or cereal was just plain boring. She had grown up with *huevos rancheros,* blue corn cakes, salsa, pinto beans, and tortillas. Now that was breakfast.

She had dressed professionally in a gray knee-length skirt, white blouse, and matching gray cotton jacket. Dark nylons disappeared into polished black pumps. As she walked out to the parking lot, she realized she missed the familiar weight of the Sig Sauer in her now too-light purse.

The black Escalade was waiting, engine running. She walked to the passenger door, opened it, and was surprised to find a sandy-haired man—moderately attractive in a rugged sort of way—sitting behind the steering wheel. He wore a light but well-tailored jacket and cotton slacks. She guessed his age at somewhere in his late thirties.

"Christal Anaya, I presume?" He reached out a firm hand. "I'm Lymon Bridges. Hop in."

She shook his hand, settling herself into the seat. He studied her for a moment through clear hazel eyes. "Have a nice flight?"

"Center seat," she told him. "I was stuck between a fat woman and her screaming child."

He grinned as he put the car into gear. "Do you always jack people around?"

"Depends."

"On what?" He waited for a gap in traffic before accelerating.

"On what I need to learn."

"So, what have you learned?"

"Your office manager is happy and loyal. That says a lot."

"I pay her to be nice to me. Some people will do anything for money."

"How much did you pay Sid?"

"If I could figure a way, I'd give him half of the federal budget." He seemed nonplussed as they stopped and started, inching along in the LA traffic. Heat mirages were dancing off the chrome and glass surrounding them.

She tried to see everything, watching the people on the sidewalks, reading the business signs. "How much did Sid tell you?"

"About you? Enough."

She started to push it, then hesitated. "Where are we off to now?"

"Meeting with the principal." He gave her that evaluative glance.

"Mel Gibson?"

"Nope. He's still in Australia pawing around among the didgeridoos looking for his lost razor." He took a right, following a winding road past sprawling white stucco houses. As they proceeded, the houses became more impressive.

"Where are we?"

"This"—Bridges gestured with the flat of his hand —"is Beverly Hills."

He took a side road into a gated community. At the security booth, Bridges rolled down the window. The guard bent, got a good look, and nodded, saying, "Good day, Mr. Bridges."

Christal noted the cameras that watched them from both sides of the gate. Then she caught the guard staring into a computer monitor as he punched in numbers. "They record the plates?"

"They do," Lymon told her as the gate slipped silently open. "And the camera behind his window recorded my face. He typed in the license as we drove up; the computer flashed my image, Paul's, June's, and the rest of my team's."

"So much for big brother." She was watching the tall walls pass as the road wound around past additional gates that led to imposing houses among the trees. "Are these people paranoid, or what?"

Lymon chuckled humorlessly. "Let's just say that the life of a superstar comes with a pretty hefty price tag."

"It's like a prison in here."

"It is indeed. Palatial, but still a prison." He pressed a button on what looked like a garage door opener, and a gate opened on a recessed drive to their left. Lymon rolled his window down again, waving at the security camera as he passed.

Christal gaped as they drove down the tree-lined lane and rounded the circle drive. Lymon stopped a short distance from a bright red Ferrari.

"Damn. Rex is here."

"Rex has a nice house." Christal stepped out, looking around at the manicured grounds. The huge three-story house was partially covered with ivy. She'd never been this close to a mansion before.

"Rex is Sheela's business manager."

"So, Sheila is the client?"

"Sheela Marks," he told her, watching her reaction.

"That Sheela Marks? *The* Sheela Marks." Then she frowned. "Some guy with a needle and a stun gun attacked her in New York. Got through her security. *Your* security. Is that what this is all about?"

He smiled for the first time, as if she'd just passed some test. "Let's go in and see what you've got."

# CHAPTER 15

"*Mr. Bridges' party is here.*" Tomaso's voice came through Sheela's intercom. "*I have placed them in the conference room.*"

Sheela pressed the button. "Thank you, Tomaso. Please see to their needs."

"Yes, ma'am."

God, she was getting tired of "yes, ma'ams." She finished toweling off, closed the shower door behind her, and walked into her closet. She picked a leisure suit by Carolina Herrera consisting of white cotton trousers, an off-white blouse, and a matching short-cut jacket. As she dressed, she wondered if Lymon would be imagining her half naked in the fitting room.

That look he had given her as she peeled out of that horrible red dress had burned right through her. Worse, she'd responded to it, surprised enough to grab the robe before walking over to speak with him.

"He's right," she muttered to herself. "It wouldn't work."

Hell, Hollywood was filled with stories of celebs who married the common folk. It always came to grief.

*I was common folk...once upon a time.*

That knowledge had begun to haunt her. Not that anything would change. She was at the top. All it took was a glance across her opulent bedroom at the golden statue that stood on the marble table beside the bed. Not bad for a farm girl from Quill Lake, Saskatchewan. Who would have believed?

She finished buttoning the blouse, slipped her feet into comfortable sandals, and headed downstairs. Checking her watch, she had two hours before she had to dress for Bernard's party. It would take nearly an hour for Paul to drive her up to Bernard's place in Laurel Canyon. Take Rex? Or have him drive separately? If he went, they could discuss strategy and tactics on the way. But that meant waiting around to bring him back. Rex was a party animal who, despite his age, didn't pay attention to normal biorhythms.

She descended the stairs and walked to the conference room. Rex sat at his usual place at the table, a glass of scotch in his hand. Lymon, according to script, was drinking coffee. She studied the raven-haired beauty beside him as everyone stood upon her entry. Midtwenties, with dark eyes that could melt a man. A very attractive woman. She had dressed professionally and carried herself well, nothing frail about her. Definitely not fluff.

She glanced curiously at Lymon. God, bringing this Latina angel wasn't some sort of macho defense mechanism, was it?

"Sorry to be late. Fitting took a little longer than we

expected." She gave Rex a smile. "But Fiona's mollified for the moment."

"I'd like you to meet Christal Anaya," Lymon said. "Christal, this is Sheela Marks."

"My pleasure," Christal said as she shook hands, the grip firm. Hard eyes met Sheela's. Good, she wasn't going to get the usual "I love your work" bullshit, or the fawning, tongue-tied admiration. But then, she wouldn't have made it this far past Lymon's penetrating radar if she wasn't professional.

"Let's get to it, shall we?" Rex said, taking his seat. "Lymon, what have you got?"

Lymon turned his attention to Christal. "A little over a week ago, Sheela was assaulted in a hallway at the St. Regis in New York. The assailant was almost able to stick some kind of needle into Sheela. He was also armed with a stun gun. When it became apparent that the attack was compromised, he dropped a flash-bang on the floor and ran. End of story. He left no clues."

Christal nodded, reaching into her purse to pull out a small notebook. "Did anyone at the hotel recognize the man?"

"No. He kept his face either averted from, or at an angle to, the security camera. A review of the previous two week's security tapes came up blank. If the place was scouted, he didn't do it in person."

"Did anyone try to do a computer enhancement on his face?"

Lymon shook his head. "It wasn't that high a priority. Sheela was unhurt. We were happy to be through with it. The police just considered it a typical prank against a celebrity. They dusted for prints, asked around the hotel, and did a preliminary investigation."

Christal jotted something in her notebook and looked up at Sheela. "You hadn't seen him anywhere before?"

"No. It was so quick. He had a dark face." She paused, frowning, wondering where the memory had come from. "He had excited eyes."

"Yeah," Lymon agreed. "Like he was victorious. Not obsessive eyes like so many fans have."

"Have you got a copy of the hotel's security tape?" Christal leaned back, frowning.

"We do. It's at the office. My people have been reviewing it, looking for ways to make sure it doesn't happen again."

"I'll want to see it." She twiddled the pen in her fingers. "I don't suppose we could get the police reports. Not just on Ms. Marks, but on the other break-ins?"

"Uh, what are we leading toward here?" Rex asked uncomfortably.

Sheela placed her palms on the table. "I want to know what happened, Rex. Lymon and I are thinking of turning Ms. Anaya loose to see what she can dig up."

All eyes went to Rex when he said, "Don't you think that's going to be a distraction?"

"From what?" Sheela cried. "They've turned *Jagged Cat* into sidewalk puke with the rewrites. Personally, after reading the latest script, I think it ought to be called *Cat Litter*. That way we might get a jump on the reviews, don't you think? A distraction? The way it's written now, I could play *Jagged Cat* half-stoned." She shook her head. "No, Rex, I *need* to know what happened in New York."

"It was some loony fan," Rex muttered.

"I don't think so," Christal said absently. She did with tone of voice what a shout couldn't. She fixed Rex's attention. "It's part of a pattern."

"What pattern?" Lymon asked.

Christal shrugged. "When I figure it out, I'll tell you."

"This is bullshit," Rex added, but he did it with less certainty.

"Humor me." Sheela used her hard look to put Rex in his place, then asked Anaya, "Tell me something about yourself."

Christal's dark eyes didn't waver. One thing about her: She didn't seem the insecure type. "There's not much to tell. I grew up in rural New Mexico, went from UNM to Princeton. After law school, I placed an application with the FBI. I worked as a special agent handling drugs, racketeering, and money laundering."

"Why did you leave?"

Christal's eyes seemed to expand, but she didn't hesitate before saying, "I got entangled in an unfortunate relationship with a fellow agent. Bad judgment on my part."

"Bad judgment?" Rex asked as he shot an *I don't believe this* look at Lymon.

Anaya was bristling, fists knotted, eyes slitted as she studied Rex as if he were some sort of insect. That, more than anything, tipped Sheela's balance. She turned on him. "As if *you* could talk, Rex." She grinned sardonically, avoiding a glance at Lymon. "As if *either* of us could!"

Lymon picked that moment to say, "I asked Christal to come out here for an interview because she has skills my people don't."

Sheela focused on the woman. "Can you do this? Figure it out on your own?"

Christal frowned down at her notepad. "Honestly, I don't know. With the Bureau, I had certain resources, people with different expertise just a phone call away."

"People with the same skills are in the private sector," Lymon replied.

"But they're expensive—" Christal started, then glanced around at the opulent room as if she had just realized what she'd said.

Sheela appreciated her modesty. "Are we talking thousands, tens of thousands, hundreds of thousands, or millions?"

"Tens of thousands," Lymon stated. He glanced at Christal. "How long do you think it will take?"

She straightened. "Wait a minute, Mr. Bridges. I haven't said I'd do it yet."

"I haven't given you the job yet, either. I just asked how long it would take."

As Christal considered, she drew little circular doodles on her pad. "Do I get a date with Mel Gibson? Assuming I can find his razor?"

"Probably not," Rex muttered.

Lymon shook his head.

"I can guarantee coffee with Sheela Marks," Sheela said dryly. "I have an in with her business manager."

Christal raised her hands, looking uncomfortable for the first time. "Mr. Bridges, I can't give you a firm commitment on the time. If it's just a single event, a fan looking for a moment's fame, maybe a week. If it's what I think, part of a pattern, then who knows? A month? Maybe more. It would depend on the complexity of the case, the resources I have available. Sometimes, hell, it can boil down to dumb luck."

She met Lymon's glance. "Sorry, that's the best I can do given the facts at hand."

"Thank you." He glanced at Sheela, then added, "Ms. Anaya, would you mind stepping out into the hall for a moment?"

Christal glanced back and forth, reading expressions, smiled professionally, and walked out, closing the door behind her.

Lymon frowned down at the table, his face a mask of indecision.

Rex blurted, "I think this is nuts!"

"You weren't there," Sheela said calmly. "You don't know what it felt like." She glanced at Lymon. "What do you think of her?"

He shrugged. "Right off the bat, I think she's smart, capable, and curious. She might be just what we're looking for."

"And this thing with the FBI?" Rex prodded. "What really happened, Lymon?"

"She was romantically involved with the AIC, uh, the agent in charge, during an active investigation. The bad guy found out and managed to get photos of them in a compromising situation. My source says that she fell on her sword to minimize the damage." Lymon smiled. "Sometimes people are just people, Rex."

Rex wasn't mollified. "Seriously, Lymon, wouldn't it be better if you just put her on a plane back to DC? We're blowing this thing out of proportion." He smiled. "Or, do you have *other* interests in the young lady? She's a nice piece."

Sheela saw Lymon's jaw harden and quickly said,

"My decision, gentlemen, is that we hire Ms. Anaya to look into the attack at the St. Regis." She tilted her head toward the door. "Lymon, would you ask her to step in, please?"

Sheela studied the woman as she returned. Anaya read the room's occupants, their expressions and body postures, with a single telling glance. She nodded at Sheela and took her seat, back straight, hands clasped, looking every inch a professional. Yes, she would do.

"Christal," Lymon began, "we would like to ask you to look into this, if you're willing."

"There are things I'll need," Anaya replied with a cautious smile. "I assume that I'll have an expense account for travel?"

Sheela nodded. "See to Ms. Anaya's concerns, Lymon. I'll expect daily reports."

"Weekly," Christal said as she drew a line across her pad. "I don't want to have to stop everything I'm doing to put together a report."

She looked up. "And another thing. I want you to understand there may not be anything to find. What happened to you in New York may be the work of a well-prepared fan. Maybe a maid was pulling a prank in Sydney. Talia Roberts's sheets might have been a practical joke."

She paused, looking from person to person. "The final thing you must understand is that if there really is some kind of purpose and pattern to these events, I have to find evidence to discover the truth. In other words, some crimes, no matter how vigorously and professionally they are investigated, remain unsolved."

"So, we could be paying you for nothing?" Rex asked as he rattled the ice in his scotch.

Christal fixed him with a piercing intensity. "No, Mr. Gerber. You will be paying me for my dedication, ability, and expertise."

Sheela decided she liked Christal Anaya. It wasn't just anybody who could feed Rex his lunch like that.

"All right, people," Sheela said, getting to her feet. "I've got an hour to prepare for Bernard's party. Rex, I'll see you there. Lymon, Ms. Anaya, thank you for coming. I'll be looking forward to your progress."

# CHAPTER 16

Bernard Antillio had attached himself to *Jagged Cat* when the studio first optioned the screenplay. He, along with Sheela, had been the leverage to green-light the picture. Bernard was considered a hot director. His last picture, *Three,* had been nominated for a Golden Globe and swept away its competition at Cannes, Toronto, and Sundance.

The guy looked the part. He had shaggy black hair that he wore over his ears like a fuzzy helmet. He left his white oversized shirt unbuttoned at the top to display a thatch of black chest hair. A narrow face, darkly complected, was home to large brown eyes that projected a brooding intensity. A good distribution deal on *Three* had not only boosted Bernard to fame, it had paid for his new digs.

The house dominated a brush-covered lot atop the mountain on Miller Drive. The structure itself looked like haphazardly stacked triangles impossibly propped up with stainless steel columns that glittered in the lights. A wag had once said the place reminded him of a pile of giant cement mousetraps that had been sprung and then filled in with glass.

From the highest of the pointed decks, one could see from La Cienega to the Valley. As Rex stood at the prow of one of the highest wedges—a combination of roof and deck—he nursed his scotch and stared out at the endless lights of the city spread so far below. They made an improbable seascape of twinkling yellow that illuminated the high clouds with a murky lemon glow.

His mind was knotted around Sheela's fixation on the New York attack. Now they had a what? A private investigator? And she would discover what? That a wacky fan had jumped at Sheela? Things like that happened. Adulation bred obsession. Stars like Sheela had to accept the lunatics, stalkers, and sycophants.

He chewed his lip, glanced back at the party visible through the windows, and listened to the music and chatter rising from the lower decks. A woman's high laughter carried over the babble of voices. They were mostly the movers and shakers from *Jagged Cat,* although the usual smattering of producers, execs, agents, stars, and wannabes had shown up. The place would have been packed but for a premier gala in Bel Air.

Glancing down two levels, he could see Sheela in her pale blue dress. People crowded around her— supplicants in search of favor from the goddess of the moment. He wondered how she was bearing up under the demands. Adulation and parasitism had a great deal in common.

He turned his attention back to the view and recalled the afternoon. Rex couldn't help but grin at the memory of Christal Anaya's rich eyes. He would dream about her for a while. She had spunk—something he didn't see very much of these days.

Bernard came walking up, a drink in his right hand, his left arm draped suggestively over a young blonde girl's shoulder. When Rex glanced at her, his first impression was of shining white teeth, vacuous beaming eyes, and tits that had absorbed too much Miracle-Gro.

"Hey, Rex," Bernard greeted, his smile that of a satisfied barracuda. "Good to see you. I hoped you'd come." He glanced over the railing at the people clustered around the bar on the lower deck. Down at ground level, a muscular young man dove cleanly into the pool. Knots and clusters of people could be seen chatting on the lower levels and through the tall windows. "Great party, huh?"

"Yeah, and if that kid working for the valet scratches my Ferrari, I'll have his liver flayed with a weed eater."

Bernard flashed his white teeth. "They've got insurance. I heard in advance that Felix was coming. Never piss off a lawyer who can afford a Bentley. Either he's very good, or he lucked into a tobacco settlement."

Rex nodded, smiling warily. "Yeah, I wanted Felix here." He pointed. Two levels down Felix was talking to Fillip Hart, the studio CFO. "As we speak, he's telling Fill that Sheela's on the way out."

"Out of what?" Bernard continued to grin, his teeth white against his dark narrow face. The blonde under his arm was beaming up at him, awe and anticipation in her wide blue eyes.

"You've read that latest crap they've written into the script?"

Bernard's eyes narrowed, and he took a slurp from his glass. The girl frowned as if suddenly confused. Bernard chuckled, apparently unsure if he wanted to fire back at Rex or if it was a joke. "Valerie, let me introduce you to Rex Gerber. Rex, Valerie."

"Hi, ya," Rex granted, lifting his scotch glass in a mock salute.

"Rex is one of the last of the true Neanderthals."

Rex grinned. "So? Let me guess. You optioned the Scott Ferris story?" The grin died. "Don't fuck with the script, Bernard. You're not good at it."

"Fuck you, Rex! *Jagged Cat* needed more punch. That's what we added. In case you haven't been paying attention, box office is where it's at. The marketing research indicates—"

"Bernard." Rex lowered his voice. "I'll tell you just what Felix is telling Fill. We're going back to the original screenplay, or Sheela's exercising her option to bug out."

"Rex, she signed the contract." It had finally soaked into Bernard's shaggy head that Rex was serious.

"She did, to do *Jagged Cat* the way it was way back when. Remember how it used to be a story instead of a blood fuck?"

"The public wants—"

"People want Sheela Marks doing what she does best. And it ain't being raped by her father before she chops him in two with a shotgun." He waved down Bernard's protest. "That's it. End. *Finis*."

Rex smiled at the girl. "Nice to meet you." He left Bernard sputtering and cursing.

He walked through the rich aroma of pot where four people sat passing a joint in the shadow of a palmetto and stepped through the sliding doors into the house. He squinted in the lights just as Tony Zell caught his eye. Tony lifted a hand and excused himself from Shinyan Seboyans's manager.

Either it was a trick of the lights, or Tony had put something in his blond hair to make it slightly iridescent. The gold chains around his tanned neck were visible inside a loose black silk shirt. Three gold rings adorned his right ear.

"Rex?" Tony greeted, taking his arm and pulling him off to the side. "Fill me in, buddy. I'm hearing stories."

"Yeah, it's true," Rex began. "Sheela's really cranked about it."

Tony made a pained face. "Why? I tell you, it's no big deal. So, it's a little publicity. It'll blow over. Not that it hurts, huh?"

"Bad publicity? I'd call it a bit more involved than that." Rex crossed his arms, looking into Tony's perplexed blue eyes. He waved away Aaron Purcell, who was walking up with a beaming smile on his thick lips. "Later, Aaron. Okay?"

"Yeah, see me." Aaron nodded happily at Tony and veered away.

"It's *not* a big thing!" Tony insisted. Then he asked, "Did Lymon put her up to this?"

Rex made a face. "What would Lymon care? And, yeah, it is a *big* thing. Sheela might be on top right now, but she's vulnerable. Women always are. She might survive one dunking, but she's not a man. She can't take two."

"Why?" Tony looked worried as he fingered the gold ring on his left index finger. "Are there threats?"

"Nothing that Felix can't handle. Look, they don't want the publicity. If they don't handle this right now, it'll be in *Daily Variety's* Monday edition. It'll be talked all over town that the screenplay's such a piece of shit that Sheela's walking. That kind of negative... What?"

"What are we talking about?" Tony looked perplexed.

*"Jagged Cat.* What the hell did you think we were talking about?"

"Sheela's walking on *Jagged Cat?"*

"Haven't you been listening? I sent you an email. Either they go back to the original story, or we're gone. Remember that clause that Felix put into the contract? We gave up two percent of box office for the right to ankle if anything pissed us off."

Tony nodded, thinking.

"What the hell were you talking about?"

"This thing at the St. Regis in New York." Tony shook his head. "I don't know why it weirded Sheela out so much. I mean, man, these things happen. She knows that."

"Yeah, well, Lymon found her a PI—a woman, no less. A real bitchin' number, too. Mexican, I'd guess. Like Jennifer Lopez, but more intense. Not J-Lo. Raquel, from the old days. Classic, with that fire in her eyes."

Tony's gaze had fixed on infinity. "She got a name?"

"Christal Anaya. Ex-FBI. Lymon gave me a thumbnail on her. She got caught fucking some of the Washington brass. They were going to kick her out, so she resigned rather than make a stink."

Tony gave him a careful scrutiny. "You think she can do anything?"

"Hell, how would I know? If you ask me, it's a waste

of money. But, yeah, if there *is* anything there, I think she's a bloodhound. She'll sniff it out."

Tony had fixed his gaze on one of the bronze statues that stood in the corner of the room. It looked like green spaghetti that dripped water.

Rex rattled the ice in his glass. "Meanwhile, you might stop and have a nice chat with Fill. Just mention that we've still got a deal with him for two pictures. Ask him what he's got in mind for a replacement if Sheela legs on JC."

Tony nodded as he fingered his gold chain. "Yeah, I'll do that." After a pause he glanced up. "FBI, huh? No shit?"

# CHAPTER 17

"Why are we here?" Christal asked as she looked around at the expensive furnishings in Morton's. The table-cloths, the centerpieces, the diners in fashionably taste-less dress, left her uneasy. Something about the young beaming staff didn't seem right to her. They hustled about with an unaccustomed alacrity, smiling, seeming to be happier than circumstances warranted. And then she got it: They were too beautiful.

"I want you to get it out of your system." Lymon waved around. "Morton's is probably the most famous restaurant in Beverly Hills. So, here you are. This after-noon you sat across the table from Sheela Marks. Tonight you're where all of Hollywood's greats either eat or have eaten."

He pointed to a booth in the back. "There's Arnold Schwarzenegger with one of his managers. As many movies are pitched, brainstormed, and green-lighted in places like this as in board rooms."

She chewed thoughtfully on her salad as she shot a

furtive glimpse at Schwarzenegger. God, the guy wasn't nearly as big as she thought he'd be. He looked older than he did in the movies. "Okay, so just what is it that I'm supposed to be learning here?"

"That once you get past all the hype, the money, and other bullshit, we're just dealing with a bunch of people. Stressed out, but still just people with all the baggage that entails. True, they're more egotistical and screwed up, but then they've got the means to support and reinforce their egotistical and screwed-upness."

"Sheela didn't seem screwed up."

"That's one of the reasons I like working for her. She still has horse sense."

"Horse sense?" Christal lifted a dark eyebrow. "Is that a bodyguard technical term?"

He stuck a fork tine into a tomato wedge. "Not yet... but it ought to be. I said horse sense because she comes from a Canadian farm where they raised horses— mares, more precisely—for urine. Some kind of estrogen source for menopausal women, or some such thing. And in the end result, you can't use the term common sense."

"Why not?"

He lifted the tomato, studying it. "Because sense is never common."

"No, I guess it isn't." The way he was looking at her made her nervous. "What is it, Lymon?"

"Did you have any training in witness protection, personal security, that kind of thing?"

"Some."

"Listen, Christal, there are four main causes of danger in the personal protection business: Intentional injury, where someone comes gunning for your principal. Unintentional injury, where the attack is targeted on someone else and Sheela just happens to be in the wrong place at the wrong time; she's collateral damage, if you will. Third are silly accidents. Say she trips over a cable while receiving an award, or maybe just slips in the bathtub."

"And the fourth?" Christal asked as she finished her salad.

"The fourth an invasion of the principal's privacy. Sheela is a very private woman that the whole world would like to keep under a fisheye lens." Lymon stabbed a chunk of romaine. "My job is to keep her safe from all four of the above-mentioned threats."

He studied her as he chewed, swallowed, and said, "Do you understand that difference?"

"What difference?"

"The difference between keeping a person safe and being a cop."

"Well, yes, I think so."

"Cops make lousy bodyguards."

"Why?" She smiled up as one of the too-pretty young men took her salad plate.

"They see trouble coming and have to stick their chins right into the middle of it. Where a cop is running in to collar the bad guy, a good personal security agent is already shepherding his principal out the back door. I want you to learn these two words, Anaya: cover and evacuate."

"Cover and evacuate," she answered. "I know that personal security is all defensive, but you hired me to dig up the reality behind these odd attacks, didn't you?"

"Yeah, but I want you to learn something about executive protection, too."

"Why?"

"Do you know how many women are in this business?"

"No."

"Damn few." He smiled. "You're going to need a job when this is all over. I want to see if you've got the right chops for a permanent position with LBA."

"I guess we'll see, won't we?" She paused. "So, what got you from the Marines to the bodyguard business?"

He had a vacant look. "I'm not sure you'd understand."

"Try me."

She wondered what lay behind those crowbar-like eyes he turned on her. "All right. It was one of those things that happen to guys who do crazy shit. You start to balance on the edge of the abyss, taunting the dragons that lurk in the deep. A good friend told me I was either going to go over or I had to get out."

"Go over how?"

"I'm an adrenaline junkie. Each mission is a high. You can be caught or killed any second. Your mind and body are so alert, so alive, it's an endorphin rush. After you are extracted, you decompress, but you no longer feel complete. Something's missing, and you can't wait for the next op so you'll be whole again. You get desperate, waiting, hoping. The more dangerous the last mission was, the more you crave the next. It got so that every time I was out of the field I had to be training. If I was on enforced R and R, I got crazy, started looking for trouble."

He tapped the side of his head. "I've got the kind of

brain that gets addicted. It's a weird personality trait. Anything I do, I have to watch myself. I keep wanting more and more. A good friend figured it out before I did. So I had to quit before I got myself—and probably some other people—killed."

"I'd think working here would be just the opposite." She indicated the glitzy surroundings. "It's artificial. Fake. Arnold over there, he's not the real world. Reality is in Peoria, or Baltimore, or Denver, or somewhere."

"You're right. I'm here for balance," he replied. "But I don't expect you to understand. Like I said earlier, it's something inside my head."

The main course appeared, the impossibly pretty waiter placing Christal's salmon on the table before stepping back for Lymon's lamb.

She picked up her fork. "You're sure it wasn't the glamorous lives of the stars? A chance to rub some of that glitter off onto your elbows?"

He chuckled before washing a cube of lamb down with red wine. "Maybe. Back in the beginning. That's another reason I like Sheela. She hasn't self-destructed yet."

"Yet?" Christal raised an eyebrow.

He watched her, those hard hazel eyes making her uncomfortable. As if he were seeing...what?

"There is an old saying." Lymon wiped his mouth on the cloth napkin. "Just before God decides to destroy you, he makes all of your wishes come true. Celebrity comes with a price, Christal. A terrible gut-wrenching cost to the body and the soul. Filmmaking is an alluring business filled with unpleasant people doing unpalatable things in an unattractive place."

"Uh, hey, boss, I don't want to rain on your parade,

but those are some pretty fancy digs that Sheela lives in."

"Yeah. The walls are nice, but they're still walls." He picked at his lamb. "She wears a collar twenty-four/seven, and it's starting to chafe. She lives surrounded by twenty-four-hour security. We have restraining orders out on three different stalkers who have tried to get into her house. One, our good friend Krissy, was carrying a scalpel and a butcher shop bone saw last time she tried to get over the wall."

"For what purpose?"

"Krissy wouldn't say exactly—just that it had something to do with making sure Sheela understood how much Krissy loved her."

"God."

"Hey, nutty fans are the easy part. You only worry about them when you wake up at three in the morning and can't get back to sleep. The press, on the other hand, has her life under a microscope. Somehow paparazzi managed to get photos of her being intimate with each of her last two male friends. The average person in the streets takes their privacy for granted. Sheela's last romance began to flower at a private resort outside of Dallas. Someone managed to get a camera into her bedroom. The next day...are you all right?"

Christal forced herself to take a breath, aware that her facial muscles had tensed and her heart was pounding. "It's nothing. But, yeah, for the record, I *do* understand. What happened? The photos came with a note? Payment for non-pub?"

"Are you kidding? This was Sheela Marks and Ronaldo de Giulio, the Italian director. There they were, the next day, splattered all over the tabloids. Front page. 'Sheela and Italian Flame Caught in Love Tryst!' It was a disaster."

Christal was scrambling to recover her thoughts. "So, someone got through your security?"

Lymon shook his head. "She'd left in de Giulio's jet. His turf, not hers. But that doesn't mean that it wouldn't have wiggled past us. Maybe someone slipped the maintenance man a couple of C notes? Or the maid was offered a new car? Cameras these days are tiny. The digital revolution makes the invasion of privacy probable rather than merely possible."

"So, what happened with de Giulio and Sheela? They still together?"

Lymon shook his head. "Different shooting schedules. He was helming in Italy; she was in Manhattan doing *Rage*. The public eye is relentless in its scrutiny. And the press coverage was all over the two of them. Probing, prying. It was easier for both of them to let it pass than to deal with the pressure."

A pause as he chewed. "Most of them work twenty hours a day, seven days a week. And social media splashes the latest thing on your iPhone twenty-four hours a day. Do you really think Sheela wanted to go up to that party at Bernard's tonight?"

"I thought all the stars did was run from one party to another." Christal speared a square of salmon.

"It's business," he answered. "Maintaining connections, being seen. It's who you know, how you look. Who you suck up to. In most professions, they call it networking. She'll be there until after two tonight. Then she'll be on the lot tomorrow morning at six to continue with the wardrobe session. At noon she has to be at La Maison for lunch with Tony, Rex, and the studio bigwigs. At three, she'll be back on the lot going through makeup and costuming for this afternoon's photo shoot for the marketing and publicity people. She'll probably be out by seven. We have her booked for a fundraiser at the Beverly Hilton at eight. She'll make it home from that by one, if she's lucky. She's due at the lot again at five the next morning to prepare for a cast reading."

He grimaced. "And it goes on, and on, and on. The worst is, she's always on stage, always having to perform for execs, producers, the press, photographers, the public. Everyone but herself. Sometimes the only private moment she has to decompress is in the limo between events."

"Doesn't she get any time off?"

"Production starts next week. She'll have a trailer on the lot so she can catch catnaps. It's noisy, small, and cramped. She won't rest until the picture's wrapped. She's a pro. She can't afford to do anything half-assed. Her performance in *Jagged Cat* has to be one hundred and ten percent. If not it could kill her. A male actor can screw up a picture without torpedoing his career. A woman can't. John Travolta still makes pictures. Kathleen Turner doesn't."

Christal gave him a skeptical look. "They pay her very well for the stress. Didn't I hear that she's getting almost thirty million for *Jagged Cat*?"

"The IRS, Revenue Canada, and the state of California take about fifty percent right off the top," Lymon began, counting it off on his fingers. "Then her people get their cut of the gross. Tony gets ten percent. Rex gets fifteen. Felix picks up another ten percent. Dot gets somewhere around two hundred grand plus expenses.

That's eighty-five percent of her gross income gone. Her accounting firm charged her two hundred and twenty thousand last year to keep it all straight. She pays somewhere in the neighborhood of three hundred and fifty thousand a year in salaries, workman's comp, FICA, and unemployment for the household staff, et cetera.

"Remember how she looked for the Oscars? By the time she shelled out for tanning, the makeup artist, manicure, facial, hair stylist, and her fashion stylist, she was into her checkbook for thirty-two grand. Just for that one night."

Christal gaped. "*Thirty-two thousand?* That's almost half of what I made for a whole year at the Bureau."

Lymon didn't blink. "Of course, she's got the physical trainers, voice and dialogue coaches. Then the caterers and research assistants all send in their invoices. Insurance runs another seventy-five thousand. She's got a whopping overhead for the maintenance of the house and grounds. She's in a time-share for the Gulfstream Three—that's five hundred fifty thousand a year." He cocked his head. "On top of that, there's security, travel, and all the other nitpicky things. When you add it all up, the lady works for every red cent—and she can't quit."

Christal frowned. "Anyone can quit."

His smile was bitter. "She's in a race just to keep her place. If she took a couple of years off, Rex—who's one of the best, even if he is an asshole—would go elsewhere. She'd have to lay off half of her staff, and she couldn't keep the house and property up. She needs that jet. What if she can't make a last-minute meeting in New York? It could cost her the leading role in her next film." A pause. "Come on, Christal. You know how much pressure it puts on you when people are depending on you. Even if it's just the agents you work with in the field. You can't fuck up. You can't let them down. If it was easy to walk out, why did you take it so hard?"

She bristled. "What makes you think I did?"

His gaze was boring into hers. "We've known each other for almost eight hours now. Long enough for me to get a glimpse of the stuff you're made out of."

She smiled at that, leaning back, relaxing. "Okay, so I took it hard. What of it?"

"So, we're here. In Morton's." He waved around at the surroundings. "What I want you to take away is a feeling for the glamor and an understanding of the celebs in this business. They pay for success with little pieces of themselves. The film industry is a meat grinder. It demands more than most people can produce, body and soul. When they start to run out of gas, someone offers a pill or a bottle, and they can keep the RPMs up for a while longer, bear the pressure for another couple of months, or weeks, or days."

"And then?"

"Crash. Rehab if they're lucky. An ambulance and an obituary in the back of *Variety* if they're not." He smiled. "Most actors aren't stable to start with."

"Not like Marine recon guys, huh?" Christal asked.

He muttered, "Shit," not unkindly. "I just want you to see beneath Sheela's skin for a moment. Get an idea of the pressure. Under all the flashbulbs, fancy dresses, and long shiny cars, the world is feeding off of her blood and sucking at her soul. Then, just when it's really getting crazy, some guy tries to stick a needle into her in New York. Why?"

"Where do you want me to start?"

"That's your call. What do you think?"

"I'd like to talk to Ensley. And what about Gibson's security people? Can you arrange that?"

"I can."

She finished her salmon. "Let me follow my nose, Lymon."

"Just don't get it snapped off, Christal."

# CHAPTER 18

Christal's morning was spent in a flurry of paperwork, processing professional credentials—which June Rosen called "dog tags"—and "interfacing" with the local law enforcement. Application was made for a concealed carry firearms permit; she was fingerprinted and photographed for the background check. Then came the W-2s, introduction to expense forms, an American Express Business Platinum card, as well as a company Visa card.

"Have you got wheels?" June asked.

"Back in the lot at Dulles." Christal considered. "I'm headed back east soon anyway."

"Rent in the meantime."

So, she had finally been dropped off at the Avis counter, where she picked up a shiny white Tahoe. She had protested for a small, compact, easy-to-park model. Instead, June had coolly asked what she would do if she was driving in the rear-blocking position and the limo had a flat. Did Christal want Sheela Marks transferring to the crowded back seat of a Neon?

Now, cut loose for the afternoon, Christal looked at her map and took a stab at honest-to-God LA traffic. While she ate a burger at Wendy's, she pondered the question of where to get started. How did she find a man who may or may not be in New York? One who had jumped at Sheela Marks and run? Someone whom the NYPD couldn't even begin to place?

Christal sorted through the sheaf of papers June had provided. She stopped at a name, frowned, and punched the number into her cell phone.

*"McGuire Publicity,"* a voice informed her.

"This is Christal Anaya for Dot."

*"I'm sorry, Ms. McGuire is out of the office. Could I take a message?"*

"Is she with Sheela?"

*"I'm sorry, I can't say. I would be happy to—"*

"I'm with Lymon Bridges Associates. I'm a special investigator working for Sheela Marks."

*"One moment please."*

The moment lasted nearly a minute.

*"Ms. Anaya? This is Dot McGuire."* Dot's voice sounded mechanical. *"How can I be of help? "*

"I'd like to ask you some questions, if you don't mind. It's about what happened in New York. Would you have any free time—"

*"We're at the lot. Photo shoot. If you'd like, we could do it this afternoon."*

Christal took down the directions, ended the conversation, and gobbled her burger. She thought DC traffic had inured her to anything. She was wrong. An hour later, she located the correct studio gate and pulled up at the security booth. The place looked like a maximum-security prison.

After flashing her new LBA ID and getting instructions from the guard, she placed a color-coded card on the dash and drove through a maze of buildings. Parking lot C-2 eluded her until she stopped a guy walking past with half of a gruesome-looking rubber corpse over his shoulder and asked for directions. After finding the parking lot, Christal got lost three times before she located door 6 in building C. Another security guard finally answered her buzz and led her through a maze of hallways into a small brightly lit set. Hammers were banging somewhere in the background behind the movable walls. The whine of power saws shearing wood made a muted cacophony.

Christal thanked the guy and stepped into the room.

Sheela Marks stood beside a broken marble column. She was dressed in sleek black leather that emphasized the sculptured curves of her body. Long, unruly locks of gleaming penny-bright hair shone on her shoulders. She was glaring in a challenging but seductive way into a battery of tripod-mounted cameras that ran the gamut from thirty-five millimeter to large-format portrait jobs with accordion bellows. Three different photographers were snapping and squinting through the lenses. A knot of people stood to one side, some with clipboards, others with gadgets that looked like light meters. Calls of "Great!" "That's fine," "Looking good!" and "Fantastic!" were being called out against the construction noise.

"Makeup!" someone shouted. "She's starting to sweat."

Lymon's words from dinner at Morton's haunted Christal's memory.

"Ms. Anaya?" A fortyish-looking woman, professional in appearance, wearing beige cotton, appeared at her elbow. She studied Christal with harried brown eyes. "I'm Dot McGuire." After introductions, Dot gestured toward Sheela, saying, "What do you think?"

"It looks hot and boring," Christal replied. "Thank you for seeing me on such short notice."

Dot crossed her arms and shrugged. "At this stage of the game, I'm just here for moral support. My job gets hectic after the last scene is in the can." She pointed to the knot of people with the clipboards. "For now, they're calling the shots, and we jump to the tune."

"What can you tell me about that day in New York?"

Dot sighed. "Hell, I don't know. What can I say? We got out of the elevator and started down the hall. Sheela and I were talking about Atlanta. She didn't want to do the spot on CNN."

"Why?"

"She was tired. We'd been on the road for three weeks."

"Promotion, right?"

"Right."

"Who sets that up?"

Dot gestured around. "The studio, mostly. It's written into the talent's contract. For *Blood Rage* Sheela had to do three weeks on the road concurrent with release. But there was an additional clause that if the pic garnered any awards—e.g., the Oscar—she'd do another three weeks during the re-release and streaming push for Netflix, Apple, and the rest."

"So, anyone in the studio would have known Sheela's schedule?"

Dot gave her a weary, blue-eyed look. "Hey, Christal, anyone on earth who knows the business could have gotten the schedule. Either through the studio, through the media outlets, from Facebook, fan sites, even through our website. Our platform is huge."

"Platform?"

"Of course. Sheela Marks is big business. We average over fifty thousand hits a day. Our stuff goes viral twice a month. Where we're shooting, what we're shooting, personal interviews, critical reviews, streaming updates, where fans can find memorabilia, that sort of thing. Last December we even did a five-hour session where Sheela answered fans' questions."

"And her tour schedule was posted there?"

"Sure." Dot frowned. "Well, within reason. I mean, we didn't post that we were staying at the St. Regis. Just that we'd be in New York and what events were scheduled. Look, social media is a cannibalistic monster that breeds on its own. Info on Sheela could have been anywhere."

Christal chewed her lip as she considered.

Someone called, "This one's a wrap!"

Sheela stepped off the dais, and two assistants led her toward the rear of the set where she disappeared between the panels.

"What are you thinking?" Dot had raised an eyebrow.

"In other words, it's not that hard to find out if Sheela's at a certain hotel. I mean, not if you know the ropes."

Dot's expression had tightened. "No, I suppose not."

"Can you go through your records, see if you received any direct communications to the hotel? Anything delivered by messenger service? Notes? Flowers. That sort of thing?"

"Sure. Sheela had alterations on one of her dresses delivered. We ordered pastrami from Katz's Deli. When I wasn't on the computer, we held interviews in her suite."

"Talking to whom?"

"Everyone, dear. Confirming CNN for Atlanta, doing follow-up on interviews, ensuring that we were on the mailing list for recordings and photos, stroking the producers in hopes that they'd book us again in the future."

"Can you remember if anyone asked specifically where you were or what your schedule was?"

"Heavens, I couldn't tell you. Probably. No, surely. It wasn't a secret. Our job is to place Sheela's smiling face in front of as many people as we can. We had a ninety-three percent awareness before the release of *Blood Rage*."

Christal glanced at the man who stepped out from the panels. He looked so familiar. It took her a moment to place him. "My god, that's Manuel de Clerk!"

Dot gave her a wry look. "He's cast as the lead opposite Sheela in *Jagged Cat*."

Christal indicated the photographers as she tried to reset her switches to professionalism. "Why are they doing this? They haven't even shot the movie yet."

"Marketing." Dot indicated the cluster of people who helped de Clerk onto the little set. Amid a babble of voices, they were arranging him this way and that on the broken column. "Most of these stills go out to the marketing and salespeople. They're preselling space in the film for advertising. Solicitations will be going to soft drink manufacturers, breweries, automakers, electronics companies, you name it. The highest bidder gets his products used as props on the set."

Christal rolled that around in her head for a moment. "So, let's say that You Betch'a Beverage outbids the competition to place their drink in Sheela Marks's hands. Could they get Sheela's itinerary?"

Dot lifted an eyebrow. "Darling, this is Hollywood. For a price, you can get *anything*. This whole town is for sale, and for the right price, all—and I do mean *all*—of the people in it can be had."

Christal nodded. "Well, since I can't have Mel Gibson, how much for Manuel de Clerk?"

Dot smiled. "As soon as they're finished, I'll be happy to take you over and introduce you." She gave Christal a calculating look. "You'd better decide now if you've got plans for later. With your looks and body, he's going to want to get up close and *very* personal."

"Just like that?"

Dot nodded soberly. "This is Manny we're talking about." A measuring pause. "You interested?"

Christal swallowed hard. "Sorry, I'm working tonight."

She stopped short, something clicking in her head. "This thing at the Hilton. This fundraiser. Was that splattered all over social media, too?"

"Heavens, yes. We'll have a crowd of fans there. They get an 'I love Sheela' button for a donation. It's a benefit for multiple sclerosis. In fact, Sheela will be dropping a couple of bills into a young lady's collection can at the door, where the crowd can see her."

People retreated from de Clerk, and Christal watched the cameras clicking and whirring as her teenage heartthrob smiled into the lenses with a beguiling sexuality.

# CHAPTER 19

"Jack? How are we doing?" Lymon spoke into his sleeve mike as Tomaso opened Sheela Marks' massive front door.

*"We're looking good, boss. Howard has given the fire doors a double-check. Someone will be stationed on each of the doors all the time. We've just finished a sweep with the hotel security. Nobody's hiding in the broom closets. We checked every nook and cranny. We didn't pry up the drain covers, but if they come up that way, we'll smell 'em first."*

"I'm at Sheela's now. Paul has the car ready. I'll call as soon as we're on route."

*"Roger that."*

Dot was trotting down the grand staircase, her purse bouncing, a leather briefcase hanging from her right hand. "Hey, Lymon."

"Dot." He gestured up the stairs. "She ready?"

Dot gave him a look that said he ought to know better. "She slept through makeup. Try to keep her from flattening her hairdo when she nods off on the way, will you?"

"Any way we can slip out of this thing early tonight?"

Dot shrugged. "It's up to her."

"She's going to hurt herself," Lymon muttered.

Dot just watched him from the corner of her eye—a knowing stare. Then she added, "She said for you to go up when you arrived. Keep her safe tonight." Dot stepped past, bursting into her fast walk as she headed for the door.

"Yeah." Lymon tapped his palm on the handrail as he climbed the stairs. He walked down the long hallway with its intricate carpet and carved molding on the doors. The white walls were hung with Southwestern art. Paintings of pueblos, rainstorms over mesas, and dark-eyed Indians stared back at him. The subject didn't quite match the decor, but what the hell, it was Sheela's. It made her happy.

He stopped, knocked twice at the master suite, and heard "Come" from within.

The latch clicked under his hand, and he walked into a large airy parlor. Several chaise lounges, an easy chair, and a small wet bar stood across from a huge wall TV. Bookcases lined the walls, packed with volumes that he knew Sheela had never had time to crack.

The arched doors that led to the master bedroom were closed. To the right, he could see into the spacious dressing room. On the wall, behind a raised barber's chair, was a rack filled with cosmetics. Two big walk-in closets were open to reveal lines of dresses. Sheela was bent over the counter, examining her face up close in the mirror. She wore a Ralph Lauren "prairie" dress that George Blodwell had talked her into. White and lacy under a short-cut Spanish-style jacket, the ensemble looked absolutely stunning in contrast to the reddish-copper of her hair.

"We're ready," Lymon called by way of greeting. His smile died when she turned to greet him. He could see the fatigue that even her expert beauticians couldn't hide.

"The studio gave in," she said wearily. "We've got the original screenplay back. Rex and Tony got them to fold." She gave him a hollow smile. "I can save this film, Lymon. I can make it work."

"I'm glad to hear that. You look like you're asleep on your feet." He asked, "Do you really have to do this?"

"My best friend from high school has MS. Yeah, I have to." She arched one of her famous eyebrows. "You really look concerned."

"It's mercenary. If you kill yourself, I've got to find another client."

"You lie well." She walked past him and into the parlor. "Tell me you rode here on your bike."

"Nope. Came in the Jaguar."

"Damn!" She turned after picking up her small beaded purse. "Wouldn't it be a rush, I mean riding up to the Hilton's front door on your BMW, dressed like this?" She struck a pose, her white dress swirling.

"The helmet would do abominable things to your hair."

"When I got into this, I should have cultivated a different image. Wild and unkempt. Why didn't I do diamonds and black leather, like Cher?"

"Doesn't suit you. How about ducking out early?"

He offered her his arm as they headed toward the door. "I'll get you home for a little real shut-eye before tomorrow."

She stopped short, tightening her grip on him. "Lymon, God, what I'd give for that. Can you do it?"

"Yeah. I promise."

"How?"

"What time do you want to leave?"

"Eleven?" She sounded so hopeful.

"I'll find you, slip up, and whisper something into your ear. You look suddenly excited, and we'll walk quietly but firmly to the door. At the risk of getting your dress stained, we'll go out through the kitchen. Paul will have the limo at the employee entrance. By the time people notice, we'll be gone. Tomaso will take messages when your phone rings off the hook all night."

She searched his eyes, reading his soul. "Do it, Lymon. Then I won't need these." She pressed two little white pills into his hand.

"Are those what I think they are?"

She shrugged. "I can't very well afford to fall asleep in my salad tonight, can I? People are paying three thousand a plate for the opportunity to eat in my presence."

Lymon tucked the pills into his pocket. "Where'd you get them?"

"A concerned and helpful friend. Does it matter?" Her lips tightened. "Come on, you know what goes down people's throats, up their noses, and into their veins at parties in this town."

"It's a one-way trip," he warned as he led her into the hall.

"I was told that those were all right. You should recognize them. Aren't they standard issue for the military?"

"Depends on the mission, but yeah. We call them 'Go' pills. Uncle Sugar thinks it's perfectly all right for a young soldier to screw with his metabolic rate when the alternative is seeing his dead body dragged naked through the streets by an angry crowd." He made a face. "Thing is, either way, the soldier is the one who ends up paying the price."

She gave him a curious glance as they started down the stairs. "Tell me, Lymon. Did you ever use any of those little pills?"

"Those and some other things you wouldn't want to know about."

"Did they work?"

Their eyes met as he said, "I'm alive today because of those little pills. They're one of the reasons I quit, Sheela. Yeah, you can stay awake. You can wring wonderful things out of your body when it's absolutely exhausted. What you've got to remember—the hitch, if you will—is that nothing comes for free. You're burning yourself, using your blood and meat and soul for fuel."

"So, what's the difference? I do that every day anyway. What's one way over the other? Maybe it's easier with pills."

Tomaso opened the door for them, bowing politely. "Good evening, ma'am."

"Thank you, Tomaso." Sheela gave him a smile.

On the steps, Lymon added, "Easier? Is it? Don't you already have enough things feeding on you?"

He held the door for her and had started to close it

when she beckoned him inside with her. "Go ahead, Paul," she called. "Lymon and I have some things to discuss."

As the car pulled away, she was frowning down at her gauzy white dress. "I want you to understand something. I've always had a strong will."

She waved him down when he started to speak. "Lymon, once, when I was fourteen, I got into trouble. Dad had an old Yamaha dirt bike he used to ride out to check the irrigation. It was missing one of the covers over the sprocket. I wasn't ever supposed to ride that motorcycle."

She leaned her head back, closing her eyes. "So, of course, once when Mom and Dad were gone to Regina for a horse auction, I got that damn bike started. The first thing I did was fall over. That chain pulled the inside of my leg right into that sprocket. It was a real mess—took a damn fortune in cosmetic surgery to fix it."

Her face had begun to relax as she looked back into the past. "I slapped a bandage on it—wrapped it in gauze we used for the horses' tails when we trailered them. God, I knew that Dad would be furious when he got home. I was scared silly about what he'd do and decided the only logical course of action was to run away from home until it healed."

She smiled. "Can you imagine that? You're not real smart at fourteen. Anyhow, I caught a ride to Saskatoon on a wheat truck. I was riding in the back. August, you know, eh? Hot. Sometime flies got under that bandage. It started stinking and itching. I was too scared to look."

He watched her throat work as she swallowed.

"The police picked me up at a Tim Horton's two days later. When they took that bandage off, I threw up."

"Maggots?" he asked softly.

She gave a slight nod. "That experience freaked me out. To this day, I can't stand flies. It's made me very protective of my body." She hugged herself. "This is all that I have left. It's the only private me that I have to myself. The whole world has the outside. It's only the inside that is still all mine."

Her fatigued eyes opened, and she gave him a miserable stare. "So, no drugs unless I just can't help it. I'll try to keep me to myself no matter what the cost."

"Let me know if I can help."

She blinked, stretching and yawning. "You just did."

# CHAPTER 20

Christal parked the Tahoe in a lot off Peninsula four blocks from the Hilton. On the long walk, she ruminated on the necessity of getting one of those parking permits from June when she finally got her car to California. Which gave her pause. Was her little squat Nissan still a prerequisite?

*Don't ditch the past until you know you can pay for it.*

Her mother's words echoed in her head as she remembered the time her father had traded in a perfectly good '99 Ford F-150 pickup for a shiny new 2013 Chevy three-quarter-ton with all the stuff you could pack into a truck. Three weeks later, his boss sacked him when he showed up for work drunk. When it was all said and done, the bank repossessed the shiny new Chevy, and Mom had to drive him around looking for another job. Six months later, she filed for divorce.

Christal frowned as she walked along the street, following in the wake of others trucking toward the Hilton. A breeze off the Pacific had sent the infamous brown cloud eastward over San Bernardino. The cool air was pleasing, not at all like the humid heat that mugged DC in the summer.

The palm trees, the brown-skinned people in low riders, the numbers of signs in Spanish reminded her of home. Truth was, LA was more like her kind of city. Sort of like Albuquerque on speed and steroids.

A crowd had already gathered at the drive into the Hilton. She stopped by the sign pointing to registration and studied the people. She wasn't sure what she was looking for. The guys with the expensive-looking camera equipment had a veteran certainty about them. Something about their body language, the way they moved, reminded her of hunters. Paparazzi, she decided.

The fans she figured for the ones with the excitement in their eyes and their smartphones clutched in anxious fingers. Finally, she figured the tourists to be the ones with the deer-in-the-headlights look. The clothes seemed to bear this out.

Mingling with the crowd, Christal just walked and listened. A number of people were wearing I LOVE SHEELA pins. She caught bits of gossip, conversation about children, lots of discussion of movies and TV programs, some sports (particularly the Angels), a new restaurant on Wilshire, and bits and pieces of gossip about celebrity social life.

"I'm just so sad," one woman was saying to her friend as they gawked down the drive, waiting for their glimpse of greatness. "De Giulio was just perfect for Sheela. God, what I'd give to have a guy like that crawl into my bed."

"He's too fast," her friend, a middle-aged woman in a pink stretch blouse, replied. "Trust me, you need a steady guy, not some slick who's gonna be sniffing out every muff in town."

Christal arched an eyebrow, remembering Lymon's description of Sheela's affair.

"Manuel de Clerk's really going to be here?" another young woman asked her friend. "I can't believe it!"

Didn't any of them have real lives? Christal thought back to the afternoon, to actually meeting de Clerk. Instead of giddy like her heart cried for, she had been professional, safe in her FBI mode.

That she had declined to give him her phone number when he asked brought home just how scarred the affair with Hank Abrams had left her. But it was more. That look in his eyes had sent a quiver down her spine. Damn it, he'd looked at her as if she was just another sure thing.

She walked on, hearing familiar names: Chris Hemsworth, Jennifer Aniston, Scarlett Johansson, Talia Roberts, Mark Wahlberg, and Kate Hudson. At curbside, fit-looking men in suits stood at ease, eyes on the crowd. Obviously security.

A cheer went up.

Christal rose on tiptoes to see a long white limo round the corner. The crowd seemed to flow down the walk to the red velvet ropes. Christal stepped back, climbed onto a cement planter, and watched—not the occupant, Ryan Williams of *Over the Streetcar* fame, who stepped out to cheers—but the crowd.

The loners immediately caught her attention. Was it the fixed expression, the posture? She could almost sense their isolation as they stood packed shoulder to shoulder with other people. Her gift had been the ability to see scars on the psyche the way others saw them on the body.

*Those are the ones to watch.*

Then a moving head marked by a red cap caught her attention. Another cheer went up as another limo came gliding down the drive. A thousand phones were held high to video the event. The waving arms reminded her of the swaying of seagrass in a current, and voices called out in giddy excitement. "Shaquille O'Neal!"

Christal had no trouble seeing him tower over the crowd as he waved and called out, "Hey! Let's all give for MS!"

Another cheer went up.

The red cap was coursing through the press of bodies, an anomaly; it worked like an advertisement. And then, glancing across, she could see a second hat slipping through the crowd on the other side of the drive.

A single shriek set the stage as a black limo came ghosting down the drive.

"Sheela Marks!" a shrill voice called.

Christal balanced on precarious tiptoes, staring over the sea of smartphones as the door opened and Lymon stepped out, his hard hazel eyes on the crowd. He glanced at the security, then reached inside to offer his hand to Sheela.

The popping strobes reminded Christal of full automatic muzzle flashes. Sheela smiled, waved, and threw a kiss to the ecstatic crowd. The roar drowned anything she said for the benefit of multiple sclerosis.

"You a Sheela Marks fan?" a voice asked.

Christal looked down, seeing one of the red hats. A

young man, perhaps twenty, dark-haired, slightly bored-looking, wore a white T-shirt stenciled with the words GENESIS ATHENA. A stack of fliers was in his hand, something photocopied on chartreuse paper.

"Yeah," she said. "Of course."

"Here." He handed her one of the papers before he turned away. She watched him walk from person to person, handing out the sheets.

She folded it between her fingers, looking back in time to see Sheela, in a lively white dress, step through the double doors; Lymon followed a step behind on the right.

By the time the last of the celebrities had arrived, teenagers were circulating through the crowds with ornately decorated coffee cans, soliciting donations.

Christal chipped in a five-dollar bill. Only then did she look down at the flashy green paper she held.

GENESIS ATHENA was prominently printed across the top.

WHAT WOULD YOU GIVE TO SHARE YOUR LIFE WITH THE IMPOSSIBLE?
GENESIS ATHENA MAKES DREAMS COME TRUE. YOU CAN BRING HER INTO YOUR LIFE.

Below the words was a picture of Sheela Marks. When Christal turned it over, the same words were written with a photo of Manuel de Clerk. A phone number and the Internet address WWW.GENESIS.ATHENA.COM were printed at the bottom.

# CHAPTER 21

Lymon locked his BMW RT, undid the D rings on his helmet, and climbed the stairs to his office. The clock in the motorcycle's fairing had told him it was six-forty. He yawned, figuring that he could sneak home before noon and nap prior to meeting Paul at the studio. They needed to finalize arrangements for Sheela's trailer.

He slipped the key into the lock and stepped inside before he hung his helmet and leather jacket on the peg in the storeroom. Equipment was stacked on the shelves, and a big gun safe lurked in the rear. Walking down the hall, he was surprised to see a light on in his office. A greater surprise was finding Christal Anaya seated at his desk. She was hunched over the computer monitor, her raven hair a jumbled mess falling over her shoulders. A half-empty cup of coffee rested to one side. Evidence she'd been there for a while. A yellow legal pad lay askew to her right as her fingers tapped keys.

"Make yourself at home."

She glanced over her shoulder; her large dark eyes might have looked right through him. "What is obsession worth?"

Lymon stepped in and walked over. "Whatever the market will bear." He flicked a finger back and forth. "You're in my chair, at my desk, using my computer."

Her gaze seemed to clear, and she looked up at him. "This is yours?"

"So, tell me, did you just make yourself at home in the SAC's office at the FBI? Or do things like your employer's privacy just not rate very highly on the Christal Anaya scale of propriety?"

A challenging eyebrow arched, and he could see fatigue behind her shapely face. "Sorry, boss man. You should put a sign on the door. I didn't know this was yours. I needed a computer. June's looked daunting at the front desk. I know this model of Apple."

He waved his finger again. "Two questions: One, what the hell are you doing on my computer? Two, how long have you been here?"

She glanced at her phone where it lay off to one side. "Shit! Is that the time?"

He noted that half the yellow pad was folded under the backing. "Start at the beginning, Christal."

She pushed back in his chair, seemingly ignorant of her continued violation of his sovereign territory. A frown incised her forehead. "Have you ever looked Sheela Marks up online? Checked out the fan sites. Wikipedia? All the chat rooms and stuff?"

"Sure. So what?"

"There's a *lot* of information. Her whole career is there. Hell, her whole life. Like that she grew up on a horse ranch in Saskatchewan. All of her films. Who she's dated. All the scandals. It took me over an hour just to skim through it. Did you know that no less than fifteen different web addresses are linked to her site?"

"You've lost me. Why is that important?"

"Because there is a whole Sheela Marks subculture on the Internet. I can take you to five different chat rooms dedicated to nothing but her. One of them, wow!"

"What does 'wow' mean?"

"The address is share-la-sheela.com. It's sick." Christal studied him. "Did Sheela ever do porn films?"

"No."

"Then the nudes they run must be AI generated. You know, they put Sheela's face on a body that looks like hers ought to. For a price—sorry, boss, but I used the company Visa—you can download an image of yourself making whoopee with Sheela. All you have to do is email a digital image of yourself—a selfie off your phone will do—and they put it on the naked guy or gal doing the dirty with Sheela. You can download it as a video and watch yourself porking away on your home big-screen TV."

Lymon experienced a souring in his gut. "What else? Anything tied to the New York attack?"

Christal took a deep breath, stretching her arms in a way that an attractive young woman with a nice body in a tight black sweater shouldn't. "Mentions of it all over social media, of course. Lots of chatter about it in the chat rooms." She made a face. "But nothing that pops out at me, you know? Most of it was 'Gee isn't it awful' mixed with 'What kind of nut would do that?' mixed with 'If I got that close, I'd tell her how wonderful she is' kinds of things."

"This site with the naked Sheela—"

"And chat room to describe the experience."

"Right. Can we find that? Figure out who visits that site?"

Christal sipped at her coffee, grimaced, and said, "Cold. Damn. But that's a great coffee machine you've got."

She put the cup down. "Let's put it like this: It's probably being run out of a little shop on a backstreet in Kuala Lumpur. You thinking about sending someone to break the guy's legs and politely request that he not do it again?"

"Something like that." It shouldn't be bothering him this much.

"If you found him, my bet is that the same program would crop up from somewhere else."

"We still get the guy."

"Want my advice?"

"Sure."

"I think the best way to handle this—God, an ex-agent, I don't believe I'm saying this!—is to put feelers out over at CIT or up at one of the tech firms up at San Jose. There's got to be someone who could write a virus, something that could be inserted into a man's photo."

He picked it up. "So when it was loaded, it would infect and destroy the program?"

"It would have to be handled with discretion."

He crossed his arms, liking Christal Anaya. "So, why would you suggest something like this?"

She tapped her notepad. "I like the lady. It pisses me off."

"You never answered the second of my questions. How long have you been here?"

She pushed back in his chair, crossed her arms. "After the crowd began to fade at the Hilton, I was intrigued. I needed a computer. Instead of going home to use my MacBook, I came here."

"You've been here all night," he noted. "Anything else that you need to report before I send you home?"

Her eyes had taken on that distant look again. "Nothing that's clear yet."

"When it comes into focus, tell me soonest. But for now, get the hell out of my chair."

She nodded, smiled at him as she collected her things, and stood. "See you, boss."

She was halfway out the door when she paused, reached into a pocket, and pulled out a bright green piece of paper. "Lymon? You ever heard of Genesis Athena?"

"Nope. Is it an escort service or a fitness spa?"

"It's neither. Sheela's site has a link, and there was a kid handing these out last night." She rattled the paper. "After I thought about it, I ran the kid down. He was hired through a temp agency. The temp agency gave him the flyers, paid him fifty bucks, and van-pooled him and the other kids handing these out to the benefit."

Lymon looked at the wild green page. "So, what did you do?"

"Like I said, it's on Sheela's website and posted on her Facebook business site. I used the hot key and took the link."

"What did you find?"

She gave him a perplexed look. "A questionnaire."

"Huh?"

"Yeah, you know, the sort that you get when you take a personality profile. It didn't make much sense, so I didn't stick around. I thought maybe you might know what it was."

"Ask Dot next time you see her. Meanwhile, get some sleep, huh?"

For long moments after she'd gone, he sat, staring absently at the computer. Then he thumbed through his old Rolodex—the idea of inputting all those names, numbers, and addresses into his contacts list had always been overwhelming. He punched a number into his iPhone and waited. At the sleep-soggy voice on the end, he said, "I don't care what time it is. I need a name. Someone discreet who can write a killer computer virus."

# CHAPTER 22

Hank Abrams pulled into the drive of his upscale tri-level home in the up-and-coming Cedar View Estates in Franconia, and sighed. His wife Marsha's red Honda SUV gleamed in its spot in front of the three-care garage, looking freshly washed and waxed. He wondered why she'd left it outside. On the other hand, he never garaged his car but depended on the occasional rainstorm to keep the white Buick Enclave clean. As to the car wash option, well, he'd had other priorities over the last couple of years.

He killed the ignition and sat for a moment, looking at the high-peaked roof of his brick-sided Colonial. Nothing they could have afforded without Martha's considerable income. The freshly watered lawn sparkled in the hot afternoon sun. Marsha insisted on perfectly manicured grass. A timed sprinkler system and an expensive lawn service kept it looking immaculate.

Hank took a deep breath, feeling the heat begin to overtake the air-conditioning. What was it? Ninety-five out there? Not nearly as hot as it was going to be in the house when he had to explain to Marsha about his transfer and demotion. Pete Wirthing had given him the news just after lunch. He'd lose a pay grade, and they were sending him to El Paso. West Texas.

Where the hell was El Paso? He'd had to look on a map. How could you get so far from anything and still be anywhere?

He opened the car door, grabbed up his briefcase, and stepped out into the sunshine. He could feel warm heat swirling around him. Clammy moisture stuck his shirt to his armpits. Was that the humidity or fear?

A month ago, he'd been a hot new star in charge of his own investigation. Christal, with her uncanny ways, had broken Gonzales wide open. All the pieces of the puzzle had started to fall into place.

He hated the sinking sensation in his gut. Every nerve in his body had turned to rubber. God, how was he going to explain this to Marsha?

*You don't mention Christal, you fool. No matter what.*

He wet his lips. "Honey, the investigation went to shit. They're blaming me. Maybe I let a piece of information slide by." To his ear, it sounded good. Hell, she knew something was wrong. She'd asked him about it before bed last night.

He watched his black shoes rising and falling on the hot white cement and stepped up to the front door. On the second try, he stabbed his key into the hole. The heavy door clicked and swung open. He slipped into the cool dimness of his house. The custom oak door shut with a finality that sent a shiver through his guts.

"Marsha? I'm home."

Silence.

He found her in the dining room, sitting across the table where she could see him walk through the arched entry. Her back was straight, her black hair pulled tight and clipped at the nape of her neck. She wore a sleeveless black pullover. A white pearl necklace that she'd bought in Paris duplicated the curve of the blouse top against her smooth chest. Her large brown eyes were smoldering, her mouth tight. He could see the muscles in her jaws, bunched and hard.

"Hank?" she asked in that silky voice of rage. "Good of you to come home again."

"Huh?" He glanced at the papers on the dark walnut table in front of her. His heart stopped, seemed to stutter, and began to pound against his chest wall. He could feel the blood draining from his face.

"Who is she?" Marsha asked in absolutely precise terms. He'd heard her use that tone when she deposed hostile witnesses. As an attorney, she had few peers and was already well on the way to a partnership at her prestigious firm.

He felt his guts sliding down inside him, ready to drop right out the bottom but for the thin wall of his abdomen. With a shaking hand, he pulled out a chair and lowered himself into it before his legs gave out.

"How...?" He swallowed hard, trying to keep his voice from quavering. "Where did you get those?"

"Manila envelope," she said softly, lifting it for him to see. "Taped to the door. My name is printed on the outside with black ink." A short silence. "You didn't answer my question. Who is she?"

"No one." At her look, he amended, "An agent. Someone under me."

"Yes." A twitch at the corner of her lips betrayed her iron control. "Very much under you, as the photos so clearly demonstrate. I'm glad to see that you are so on top of your duty."

"Marsha, don't. You have no idea how hard it's been."

"Apparently she knows how *hard* it's been, Hank." Marsha slapped the photos on the table. "So, come on, spill it. Got anything to say? Perhaps starting with the reason you decided to end our life together this way?"

He lowered his eyes and rubbed his sweaty hands together between his knees. "What do you want me to do?"

As the long silence passed, he stared miserably at his hands. They looked white and weak. He couldn't nerve himself to look her in the eyes. Wouldn't be able to stand what he'd see there.

Her voice was cool. "I've taken the liberty of making a reservation for you at the Best Western. You know the one. Just before you get on the Belt Loop. I'll have your things packed by the end of the week. That allows you time to determine where to have them sent."

"El Paso," he muttered. "Send them to El Paso."

"Hank?"

"Yes."

"One last word of advice. Hire a *very* good lawyer."

# CHAPTER 23

Christal cranked an eye open, cursing the damn fool who wouldn't answer the knock at his door. The pounding came again, and she realized, to her chagrin, that it was her own door.

She flipped the covers off, fumbled for an extra long T-shirt, and pulled it over her shoulders. She pressed a hand against her full bladder, promising that it wouldn't be long.

She trotted down the stairs in the half-light and squinted as she put her eye to the door peephole. She could see Lymon's face peering back, the nose distorted out of proportion by the small lens.

As he began another spate of knocking, she pulled the door open, flinching against the bright sunlight.

"Yeah?"

"Got a moment?" He stepped past her, a serious Dot McGuire walking behind. The woman's face was a study of upset and irritation.

"Do come on in," she said to their backs and took one last glance out at the day. From the angle of the sun, it had to be late afternoon. Closing the door, she walked over and cranked the curtains open. Lymon had walked straight into the kitchen, checked the coffee machine, and pushed the button.

"Good work, Christal," he called. "We thought we ought to have a meeting."

"It's..." She frowned. "What time is it?"

"It's Hollywood, darling," Dot drawled as she pulled off her shoes and flopped into the easy chair. She tucked her nylon-clad legs under the knee-length skirt she was wearing.

"Can I get dressed?"

"Go for it. We're burning daylight," Lymon called from the kitchen.

Christal headed for the stairs. "Burning daylight? God, do people really say that?"

His shout interrupted her reverie. "Christal, dress formal. Black is preferred. Sequins acceptable. You're working tonight."

"Formal, right." She made her way back up the stairs, locked herself in the bathroom, and made peace with her bladder. By the time she had washed her face, found her best dress, and gotten most of herself together, she could smell coffee wafting up the stairs.

Lymon was perched on the sofa, a cup of steaming coffee on the low table in front of him. The television across the room was on CNN. Dot's eyes were fixed on it.

Christal poured a cup of coffee and strode in, seating herself at the end of the sofa, the cup cradled in her hand. "I take it this isn't a social call?"

Dot had raised a hand, then looked her way as a

commercial aired. "Someone hit Sandra Bullock last night."

"Is she okay?" Christal asked. "Did they get the guy who assaulted her?"

"Not hit as in hit," Lymon explained. "Hit, as in invaded her privacy and stole her toothbrush and hankies."

"Hankies? Toothbrush?" Christal realized she was still sleep-deprived.

"I mean, what's it all about?" Dot asked summarily. "Silly burglaries of people in the big twenty club."

"All right, I'll bite." Christal looked back and forth between them. "What's the big twenty club?"

"The twenty-million club," Lymon supplied. "Actors who can demand over twenty million per film. Three of them: Talia Roberts, Sheela Marks, and now Bullock have been...what? Attacked? Robbed? What do we call this, and why's it happening? Like Mel Gibson's razor. What's the point?"

"Tell me about the hankies." Christal leaned back, frowning.

"Sandy has a cold," Dot explained. "I talked to her publicity department. She was taking a long weekend at her house in Jackson Hole. Someone came in through the bathroom window in the middle of the night. Neutralized the security system and was actually in the room with her. Scared her to death. A voice called 'Good night' out of the darkness and woke her up."

"Teton County sheriff's office was there within twenty minutes," Lymon added. "They found nothing."

"They won't," Christal answered, not quite realizing why she said it.

"Why?" Lymon leaned forward.

"Just a hunch," she muttered, covering.

"Like the social media stuff?" Dot asked. "Lymon called first thing this morning. My people have been clicking on the links that have been added. We had no idea the sites could take you so many places."

"Did you find the 'hump-a-Sheela' site?" She glanced cautiously at Lymon. God, the guy really had a case for his client. Was that good, given his position?

Lymon grinned unpleasantly. "It's being taken care of. It took a couple of phone calls, but by this evening, we should be instituting countermeasures."

"I don't want to know about it," Dot said, sticking her fingers into her ears. But she went right on, saying, "We were shocked that someone could use AI to do that."

"If it was done once," Christal reminded, "it can pop up again at any time."

"I've got one of my staff detailed to spend a half day a week just following the traffic, you might say. Our webmaster has been given the go-ahead to do a more thorough breakdown of who accesses the site, where they're from, and all the other statistics."

"How about the links?"

"Legit. As you know, most are studio links that take you to film information, then there are the fan clubs, and the others are charities." Dot clapped her hands.

"What's Genesis Athena?" Christal asked.

"We don't know." Dot frowned. "They actually paid us for the link, can you imagine? We get three thousand a month. I looked at their site. All I found was a questionnaire. I assume they're some sort of marketing research company."

"But you don't know?" Christal sipped her coffee.

"Well, for three thousand a month, they couldn't be too shady." Dot shrugged. "I checked. They're linked to other stars, too. We're not the only ones."

"Like who?"

"Manuel de Clerk, for one. Then there's Roberts, Gibson, Johansson, most of the A-list." Dot ignored the news as it came on again. A story about airport security.

"But nobody knows what Genesis Athena is?"

"It's a questionnaire," Dot repeated.

Lymon was watching Christal, a slight frown marring his forehead. "Is this another of your famous hunches?"

She tapped her coffee cup with a fingernail. "I'd just find out who was using my social media platform, that's all."

"Right." Lymon nodded to Dot as if to say, "Do it."

Dot missed it, musing, "Why would they take Sandy's toothbrush and used Kleenex tissues?"

"Always something personal. Like a *brujo* would take," Christal murmured to herself.

"A what? What's a brew-ho?" Lymon asked.

She smiled sheepishly. "It's superstition. *Un brujo* is a witch. Where I grew up, the older people still believed in witches. Hell, people even suspected my grandmother. Said she had powers. That she could see into men's souls."

"Right, like the Shadow? With the ability to cloud men's minds?" Dot asked, raising an eyebrow. "I remember the movie with Alec Baldwin."

Lymon's hazel eyes probed again.

"It's nothing." Christal tried to wave it off. "Have you had time to talk to—"

"No," Lymon interrupted. "I want to hear this. How did she see into souls?"

Christal winced. "Look, it's just old superstition, huh? Backcountry New Mexico is full of it. Grandma wasn't a witch anyway, she was a healer, a *curandera*."

Dot obviously wasn't buying any of it, but Lymon had leaned forward. "What about the personal items? You said what? That a witch would take things like that?"

Trapped, she admitted, "Well, yeah. If you're going to hurt someone, you need to possess a piece of them. A lock of hair, a fingernail clipping. Menstrual cloths were really big. So was a man's semen, assuming you could get it."

She stopped, feeling something nibbling at the edges of her consciousness.

"What?" Lymon asked.

Christal shook her head. "I don't know. It's as if something's just out there, something I can't quite grasp."

"About witches? You think all these A-list actors were witched?"

"No." She tried to grasp the idea that lay just beyond her thoughts. "But that's on the right track. It's got something to do with possession."

"Bullshit!" Dot exploded. "You're not suggesting that we go to Madam Toulouse for a reading, are you?"

"God, no," Christal shot back. "I don't believe in that crap either. No, this is something that will make perfect sense when the right pieces fall into place."

Dot was building up to say something when Lymon waved her down. "Go with it, Christal. Hell, you've been here for twenty-four hours, and we've already got results."

"What?" Dot asked. "We'd have found that shit on the platform eventually."

Lymon wondered, "But would we have dealt with it as effectively?"

"Hey!" Christal straightened. "You didn't take my advice, did you? I was dead tired. Not thinking."

Lymon gave her a soldier's grin. "Hey, yourself, Chris. This is the private sector. You're not a fed anymore. You get paid for results here. It would have been such a pain in the ass to travel all the way to Kuala Lumpur to bust the guy's legs and then have to speak politely to him. It would have hurt my facial muscles."

"Right. Glad to be of service, but the laws that control—"

"Come on, Christal." Lymon headed for the door. "We don't have time to chat. We're almost late as it is."

Then he glanced at her dress, a black pullover she'd ordered from J. Crew. "You call that formal?"

"It's be that I've—"

"Shit. We've got less time than I thought. We're making a quick stop at a boutique on Rodeo Drive. When I mean formal, I mean *formal*!"

"But, I—"

"Where do you think you're living? Disneyland?"

"No, Boss. That's over in Anaheim."

# CHAPTER 24

With fingertips, Hank Abrams drew designs in the moist surface of the glass. The bar's soft lighting cast amber tones through the bourbon. The tremble had left his hands. He still hated the fact that he'd had them.

Self-loathing was a terrible thing. He didn't understand it. Ever since Marsha had thrown him out of the house, he'd wanted to hurt himself. To take something jagged and sharp—a broken bottle, twisted rusty tin—and rake his arms and chest. He wanted to sting and bleed.

*God, we're fucked-up creatures!*

He stared at his fingers as they traced figure eights on the sweating tumbler and tried to ignore the bar sounds: The barely audible announcer calling the Cleveland and Denver Rockies game on TV. Patrons were conversing in low tones, laughing. A table of men no more than two steps away were talking football. He fumed at the easy jocularity in their voices. They still had lives. Homes, wives, jobs to return to.

His eyes narrowed, remembering Christal. Her gaze was locked with his, smoky and challenging. He could remember the light in her ink-black hair, the set of her sharp cheeks. Narrow at the waist, she filled a pair of jeans perfectly. God, he'd wanted her from the moment he'd first seen her.

*Enough to totally fuck up your life?*

It shouldn't have happened that way. Hell, it had just been the two of them in the surveillance van. How had anyone been able to get pictures? Who would have known they'd fuck that night? It had been the first time —the only time. Nothing planned, really—it had just happened. As if the moon and stars had been in the right alignment.

In his misery, he'd remained unaware of the man. Surprised, he looked up to see a thin, dark-complected face, thick black eyebrows, a narrow nose, and terse mouth. The guy wore a fedora and a dark suit coat. His eyes looked like black marbles.

"Yeah?" Hank asked.

"May I sit?" The guy indicated the other chair.

"Uh, I'd appreciate it if you took one of those tables over there." He pointed across the bar. "Got someone coming, you know?"

The man's eyes never left Hank's as he pulled out the chair and sat. "You look like a man looking for a job."

On the verge of telling Fedora to fuck off, Hank hesitated. "And just what makes you think that?"

Fedora shrugged.

Hank flicked a finger to indicate the hat. "That's a little dated, isn't it? If you're trying to look like a 1930s gangster, you've got the part down pat. But for the twenty-first century, it makes you look a little hokey."

"I am Salim, Mr. Abrams."

Hank's alarm bells began going off. He straightened. "Just how the hell would you know my name?"

"A mutual friend." Salim smiled. "For the moment his name need not concern us. Let us just say that he thinks you got a bum rap. He contacted me about your situation."

"And when I find out who, I'm going to bust his ass," Hank muttered darkly. "I *don't* need any son of a bitch fucking with my life just now. And I sure as hell don't need you and whatever your scheme is. I've got enough trouble."

Salim smiled. "I have no scheme, Mr. Abrams. I come to offer you a job." He touched the tips of his fingers together. "My sources tell me that you had Gonzales, but for an unfortunate circumstance. We were impressed by that."

Hank tightened his fingers around his glass. "You want to know something? Your loudmouthed friend in the Bureau is going to get his balls chopped off one of these days."

Salim shrugged. "Where are they going to transfer you to?"

"Why should I talk to you?" Even through the slight buzz, his cop's instincts were vibrating. "In fact, why shouldn't I just pick up the phone and call a couple of friends of mine? Here you are, whack, right out of the blue, knowing all about me and no doubt about to pitch something that's too good to be true. Why do I smell shit?"

Salim smiled thinly. "This isn't a movie, Special

Agent Abrams. I do not represent a drug cartel or money laundering ring looking to exploit a down-on-his-luck agent. Here's my card." He flipped out a business card. "Take some time. Do some research—through the Bureau, if you'd like."

Hank narrowed his eyes, feeling the tingle around his senses. Wishing now that the guy had shown up two drinks ago before the bourbon had slipped its muzzy fingers through his brain.

The card proclaimed VERELE SECURITY. It gave a New York City address and phone with an email address.

"Security, huh?"

"We're licensed and registered. We specialize in executive protection." Salim gave him a faint smile. "We work for the good guys, too."

"So, why come to me?"

"Let me return to my question: Where are they transferring you to?"

"El Paso. You ever been to El Paso?"

Salim shook his head.

"Me neither. But, shit, I guess I'm going." He glanced up. "You know where I live?"

"I have your address. When I called there, Mrs. Abrams said she didn't know where you were, or care, for that matter."

"Right."

"Your personal relations do not concern me. I've been sent to see if you'd be interested in executive security. Hiring people is never hard. Local police will generally work for us when they're off-duty. But finding *good* people is always a challenge. Depending on your capabilities, the wages can be quite rewarding.

And, well, how do I say this, the environment will be a great deal more salubrious than in El Paso."

Suspicion bubbled up in his blood. First the photos were taped to his door for Marsha to find. Now this guy shows up? It tasted like an ambush to him, but who was the leak in the Bureau?

"Before I go any further, I need to know who sent you to me."

Salim studied him for a moment, the brown eyes sharp. "Fair enough. The assistant director. For reasons that I would hope you could understand, we would appreciate your discretion in this matter. Please don't charge into his office tomorrow morning demanding at the top of your lungs to know if he referred you to us."

Hank frowned. "The AD? The guy who just canned my ass?"

Salim sat back and removed his hat. "Agent Abrams, you have been around long enough to know that good people are often caught in situations that spiral out of control. The Gonzales case is one of those. As to how that camera got placed in the van, who knows? Gonzales didn't get to where he is by being an idiot. He knew you were closing in, and he fought back."

The man lifted a thoughtful eyebrow. "It's only a guess, Mr. Abrams, but I'd say that all things in perspective, professionally destroying you and Agent Anaya was his only way out. Gonzales wanted you beaten and broken...with your personal and professional lives destroyed."

Had Gonzales sent the photos to Marsha just like he'd sent them to Peter Wirthing? They'd been in a plain manila envelope labeled in black ink. Both times. "I'll get the son of a bitch in the end."

Salim waited in respectful silence, then said, "Not from El Paso, you won't. And not through the Bureau. He's wise to you."

"Is that why you hunted me down? Because of Gonzales?"

"No. I'm here because you are a highly trained agent with skills that my company could use. As far as Mr. Gonzales is concerned, you and he were playing a very high-stakes game. A smart man understands that. That he managed to exploit such a minor weakness is an example of not only his skill but yours. You can let what happened crawl around under your skin until you end up broken, bitter, and ruined, or you can accept that at this time and place, Mr. Gonzales squeaked out the narrowest of victories. Your choice is to drown in self-pity or go on to bigger and better things."

"Which you are here to provide."

"Maybe. I haven't made up my mind yet. And the final decision will rest with my boss in New York. You're half drunk, surly, and depressed."

"What do you pay?"

"If you can convince us that you are worth it, we would start your salary at eighty thousand a year. Please remember the *if* in that sentence. You must prove your worth. If you've got chops, it would rise. Security supervisors in my company make between one fifty and two fifty a year."

Salim smiled. "That, of course, does not include any gratuities that our clients might feel obligated to bestow upon you for services rendered. Our clients include some of the richest men in the world. To some of them, a twenty-thousand-dollar tip is but a pittance."

"And all I have to do is sign on the bottom line?"

"It would depend on if you could satisfy my employer and me. Tell me, Agent Abrams, are you really any good, or are you a fuckup? Answer that question honestly. If you're the first, come look us up. If you're the latter, go to El Paso, bury yourself, and don't waste either our time or your superiors'." He stood, slipping his hat onto his head. "Good evening."

Hank Abrams watched him walk away, stunned and, truth be told, curious.

# CHAPTER 25

*So, here I am, watchdog instead of wolf.*

The notion rolled around in Christal's head as she stood in the Beverly Wilshire ballroom and studied the 'beautiful people." She glanced down again at the stunning black silk Escada dress she was wearing. A block down Rodeo Drive, Lymon had parked the Escalade at the curb, lights flashing.

He'd whisked Christal in the front door. Glanced around, and pointed at the black formal on the maniken. "That one. It's loose enough you can move. Run if you have to. And no one will think you're a refugee from Walmart."

She'd looked at the tag, gaped, and turned back just as Lymon was telling the clerk, "I think she needs a size larger." And back to Christal, the finger pointing again. "The dressing room's that way."

So it took a dress two sizes bigger? The thing had already been paid for by the time she stepped out for Lymon to see. The clerk barely had time to get the tags off before they were out the door and back in the gleaming black Escalade.

Sid had been right. There was life after falling on the sword. If she'd gone to war with the Bureau, she'd have been up to her neck in lawyers, facing public instead of just professional humiliation, and making nowhere near three hundred dollars a day to stand around a plush ballroom at the Regent Beverly Wilshire Hotel wearing a brand new five-thousand dollar designer dress while trying to place names to faces she'd seen at the Cineplex down from her Virginia apartment.

"It's simple," Lymon had explained to her. "All you have to do is keep an eye on Sheela. Nothing intrusive, just be close. Guests will be screened at the door, of course, and the hotel has its house security on alert. We're just backup. Howard and Jack worked a complete advance last night. You'll be there with me, Salvatore, and Wu."

Salvatore fit the bill for the old adage of tall, dark, and handsome; he had a strong jaw and fierce brown eyes. She figured him for his midthirties, really fit, with a bodybuilder's physique. If he hadn't been a football jock in college, she couldn't guess them. He worked part-time for LBA. His day job, if you could call it that, was security for a software company in Venice where he worked four ten-hour shifts a week.

Wu was short for Yan Zan Wu, a barrel-chested Chinese guy, late-twenties, with a round and appropriately inscrutable face. He made her think of Odd Job in the Goldfinger movie until she discovered he worked part-time for LBA, too, while he finished his PhD in physics at UCLA.

As Christal tagged along in Sheela's wake, she tried not to look conspicuous and shot lethal glances in Lymon's direction. He was orbiting off Sheela's left, never more than five quick paces away. Christal figured she could kill him later. She felt like a dolt being the only woman in the room except for a bald female rock star, whose name she'd missed, without at least the benefit of blush.

In contrast, Sheela looked ravishing in a white Narciso Rodriguez dress that complemented her red-blond hair. Her face had been made up with Paula Dorf powder, iridescent eyeliner, and apricot lip gloss.

"So, you're the fed?" a blond man interrupted her pique as he stepped up to her side.

"Excuse me?" Christal took his measure: Blond, athletic, and tanned, he looked really good. She liked the sparkle in his blue eyes and the nonaggressive smile. Damn! The guy had enough gold hung around his neck to lure Coronado back from the grave.

"You don't look like a federal agent," he added, the smile displaying nice teeth.

"Do I know you?"

"Not yet. I'm Tony Zell." He offered his hand, adding, "Sheela's agent."

"Christal Anaya. Lymon Bridges Associates." She took a step to close the distance to Sheela. "I'm the FNG."

"FNG?" He looked confused.

"Fresh new girl," she punned, watching to see if he got it. He didn't, and she was unsure what to make of that.

"You're supposed to find out what happened to Sheela in New York."

"You don't sound enthusiastic about that."

He shrugged, waving at someone who called, "Hiya Tony" then said, "I don't know. I'm in the minority. It was probably just a fan getting his kicks. Bragging rights, you know?"

"He hasn't been bragging yet," she said, walking slowly as Sheela moved. How did the woman do it? Sheela's smile never wavered. She seemed to know everyone, and a genuine excitement sparkled in her blue eyes. Every movement was poised, graceful, and sinuous.

"What? So, you've been to every bar in New York?"

She arched an eyebrow. "What makes you think New York?"

"Well, that's where it happened."

"Yeah, maybe."

"What do you mean, maybe? That's where Sheela got mugged, right?"

"Sheela's not the only celeb involved here."

He glanced around, adding, "Uh, it's not my place to judge, but what exactly are you doing here?"

"Working," she added pleasantly as she led him another step, keeping her distance from Sheela's knot of people. "Lymon wants me to familiarize myself with this aspect of the business."

"You don't look anything like what a female FBI agent should look like." He snagged two flutes of champagne from a passing tray, extending one in her direction.

"Sorry, I'm on duty. Apparently you didn't see *Miss Congeniality,* or you'd know FBI agents can come in all sizes and shapes."

He laughed at that, still offering the champagne flute. "Here, at least hold it. You'll make me feel better."

She took it, looking past him, trying to concentrate on the people hovering around Sheela.

After sipping his drink, he asked, "Why do I get the feeling that you're only half here?"

"Because I'm on the job, Mr. Zell. Having you here, acting like we're having a discussion, removes attention from me. Therefore you're welcome to walk with me, assuming you don't get tired of talking to a wallflower."

"So, are you, like, always on the job?"

"They're paying me too much to waste precious time on myself."

"Hey, you've got to eat and sleep sometimes."

"Mr. Bridges doesn't seem to think so. He has developed this annoying habit of calling me at odd hours."

He seemed to digest that for a moment. "You ever think of films? Acting, I mean. You might try a screen test sometime."

That broke her concentration, and she stared flatly at him. "What? Are you kidding?"

He gave her an offhanded shrug. "I'm an agent. I'm always looking for new people. It's what I do. It wouldn't hurt to try. Talent comes from strange places. You're a beautiful woman..." He made a face as if searching for the right word. "Moxie. That's it. You've got moxie, a certain chutzpah that gives you presence."

She grinned crookedly before returning her attention to Sheela. "Are you hitting on me, Mr. Zell?"

"No." He backtracked too fast, adding to her amusement. "I'm serious about the screen test."

The auburn-haired woman caught Christal's attention. She couldn't have said why—just a quality in the woman's eyes, the way she moved. Call it predatory. Christal estimated her at five-foot-seven, tanned, with a classic Nordic face and burnished hair that streaked into sun-bleached yellow highlights. She wore a copper-colored form-fitting pantsuit that emphasized her muscular body. Skin-tight gloves covered her hands, and she held a flat purse the size of a hardback novel. More to the point, her serious gray eyes had fixed on Sheela with a feline intensity.

"Excuse me, Mr. Zell." She handed him back the untouched champagne.

He turned, following her gaze, and took a moment to study the woman. "Quite a number." He paused, and she could feel his gaze when it returned to her. "What is it about her that makes you nervous?"

"Just a hunch."

Christal stepped around a knot of tuxedo-dressed men and smiled when one asked, "Hey, Tony! Who's this?"

"Business associate," he answered smoothly. "I'll introduce you later."

The copper-headed woman had moved, calmly dismissing a young man who tried to talk to her. Bingo. She wasn't just socializing.

At that moment Sheela said something to the people surrounding her, gave them a gracious smile, and stepped away from her party. She clutched her handbag, walking purposely toward the women's restroom. Salvatore had picked her up, shadowing her right flank.

To Christal's surprise, Copperhead—as she'd tagged the woman—seemed to anticipate it and stepped into the ladies' room door a good ten seconds ahead of Sheela.

"Mr. Zell, it's been nice chatting with you."

"Hey"—he gestured with the untouched champagne—"I don't want to be a nuisance, but maybe dinner sometime? Nothing serious, just a chance—"

"Sure."

Salvatore had posted himself at one side to wait. He seemed completely at ease.

"Hole in your security, Lymon," Christal muttered as she skipped quickly to catch the door as it swung shut behind Sheela. Bright lights, mirrors, and red velvet-covered benches furnished the powder room. The three women who sat there seemed oblivious, patting and painting, applying lipstick amid the usual facial gyrations as they gazed into the mirrors.

Copperhead was nowhere in sight.

Sheela walked through the archway that separated the powder room from the toilets. Christal was two seconds behind her. Passing into the toilets, she found her quarry.

To her surprise, a short line waited: two women, Copperhead, then Sheela, and finally her. Bending at the waist, Christal assured herself that feet filled every stall.

"God," the first woman in line muttered. "This is taking forever."

"Nice reception, don't you think?" Copperhead turned to Sheela.

"Yes, it is."

"Sheela Marks, right?"

"Right. And you are?"

"Cindy Denton. I work with MCA, rights depart-

166 • W. MICHAEL GEAR

ment." She hesitated. "I liked *Blood Rage.* Saw it last week."

Copperhead was giving Christal a thorough scrutiny. Christal didn't make eye contact but fumbled with her purse for a distraction.

"Thanks, it was a fun film to make."

"Congratulations on the Oscar."

The toilet flushed, and a harried woman stepped out, pulling her skirt straight as she headed for the sinks.

"I wasn't expecting it," Sheela answered. "You always hope, but when it came, I just couldn't even think straight."

One by one, the line moved up. Copperhead stepped into the stall. Sheela glanced at Christal just as the woman in the adjoining stall flushed and stepped out. She was a mousy thing. Thin, dark-haired; the glance she gave Sheela was curious, evaluative.

Christal watched Sheela step in and close the door. She could hear fabric slough, a purse snapping, urine, then a flush. Another flush. Then another.

Finally, Sheela stepped out, pulled her dress straight, and shrugged as she walked past. Christal glanced into the stall. A tampon floated in reddened urine.

Copperhead stepped out unexpectedly, saying, "Excuse me. Please use that one." She pointed at the stall she'd just vacated as she pushed into Sheela's and flipped the door closed.

Christal stopped short. *What the hell?*

Sheela was at one of the sinks, bent to wash her hands as she checked herself in the mirror. The sounds from the stall made no sense: the lid clunking as it was lifted. Then what? Christal couldn't place the noise as she pushed on the locked door. Was that plastic crackling and dripping water?

Moments later, Copperhead opened the door, surprised when she found Christal still standing there. Their eyes locked, and Christal started forward, saying, "One moment, please."

Copperhead crouched, lowering her shoulder. She caught Christal off guard, driving her body back, off balance. Christal clawed for balance as Copperhead slammed her into the wall, then followed up with a hard blow to the solar plexus. Then another. And another.

Christal windmilled against the tiles as she tried to catch her balance. Her body jerked against the blows. She was gasping for breath, and then Copperhead was off, leaving at a run.

"Stop her!" Christal croaked, coughing as she pushed herself upright. Her guts were on fire. A glance showed her that the toilet bowl was white, the water clear.

Sheela and the other women had turned around to stare in disbelief as Copperhead ran past. The purse in the woman's hand was larger and gripped as if it contained diamonds rather than a used tampon and urine.

Christal coughed again. Her lungs burned as she drew a breath and stumbled toward the door. She straight-armed a surprised woman who stepped into her way, pounded past the alarmed gazes of the women in the powder room, and smashed the door open. Salvatore was walking toward her, concern on his face.

"The woman!" Christal croaked, still out of breath.

Then she saw her, that streaked-auburn head making straight through the crowd for the fire exit. "Stop her!"

Salvatore lifted his arm and spoke into the mike, a frown on his face. Christal forced herself forward, weaving through the surprised crowd. Across the packed room, a fire door swung open. An alarm blared flatly.

Christal could hear Salvatore's feet thudding behind her as she dodged, weaved, and shoved people out of her way. The fire door clicked closed just as she bowled past the last of the gawking spectators and hammered her body against the crash bar. She might have hit a wall. Even the impact of Salvatore's thick body didn't budge it. For a long moment they hung there, thrusting, both of them, while the alarm blared its obnoxious wail.

# CHAPTER 26

Lieutenant Harris of the Los Angeles Police Department studied the rubber wedge inside the plastic Ziploc he held. The item of interest was a door stop, one of nearly thirty scattered around the hotel. They'd pried this one out of the fire door. "Who knows, maybe we'll get a print off it. Maybe it will even be from someone who doesn't work at the hotel."

"Don't get your hopes up." Heedless of her expensive Escada dress, Christal had her butt propped on one of the wood-veneer tables as she looked around the small conference room. The walls were finished in beige and illuminated by overhead fluorescent panels. A podium stood in one corner; an easel with marketing diagrams had been left behind by some of the room's previous occupants. Outside, the press of media could be heard as two cops held them at bay in the hotel hallway.

Lymon stood with his arms crossed. The lieutenant and another detective sat at the table with the baggie.

Sheela looked shocked and humiliated as she twisted her hands in her lap. The expensive Narciso Rodriguez dress seemed to shimmer in the light. Salvatore had a chastened look, as if he'd just come up impotent on his wedding night. For her part, Christal hugged her sore stomach and fumed.

"Why's that?" the lieutenant asked.

"It was too well planned. Right down to the fake legs in the stalls." Christal pointed her chin at the plastic trash bags full of shoe-covered mannequin legs. "Copperhead was wearing gloves. You're not going to lift anything from the women's room stalls or the fake legs, either."

"How can you be so sure?"

"Did you get anything at Talia Roberts'?" Lymon asked, picking up the threads. "How about at any of the other A-listers who have had high-profile personal items stolen over the last couple of weeks?"

"You're saying this is related?" Harris looked from one to the other.

"Yeah." Christal took in the shocked expression on Sheela's face. The woman looked as if she'd just been raped. Maybe without the physical brutality, but the sense of psychological violation and humiliation reflected in her expression made Christal's heart ache. "They didn't get their sample in New York. They had to come back."

"What? What sample?"

"Their piece of Sheela," Christal added.

Harris and Lymon both turned frowns toward Christal; the former asked, "What piece are we talking about?"

"A piece of her, a bit of Sheela."

"For what purpose?"

"We don't know," Lymon muttered.

A cop opened the door and leaned in, accompanied by the sounds of melee in the hallway. "Lieutenant, there's no Cindy Denton at MCA. Not in the rights department, not anywhere."

"Thanks."

Christal could see a crush of reporters held back from the door by a small knot of police personnel. They were calling questions as the cop pulled the door closed behind him.

Harris stared at the plastic trash bags full of fake legs on the floor. "Look, even if we figure this out, we're not going to be able to do much." He met their eyes sympathetically. "What's the crime? Theft of a tampon and urine?"

"Second-degree assault," Christal replied. "She hammered me three times after she shoved me against the wall."

He studied her thoughtfully. "We'll file it that way if you're willing to press charges, but if it ever comes to court..."

"Yeah, yeah, I know. There's a hundred ways a good attorney could get an acquittal." She made a helpless gesture. "But what else have we got?"

For a moment, no one spoke.

Harris made a decision. "Ms. Anaya, we'll be sending a detective by tomorrow with a forensic artist and an old-fashioned mug book. It's obvious that the mousy woman and Copperhead, as you call her, were working together on this. If these things keep happening—"

"They will."

"—then at least we're doing something that might be proactive."

"How's the situation out there?" Sheela asked, looking sick to her stomach.

Lymon replied gently, "This has a bad smell, so the press has come in a swarm."

Sheela closed her eyes, color draining from her cheeks. Christal stepped forward instinctively and reached out. At her touch, Sheela looked up and gave a brief shake of her head, raising an arm to stop her. "It's okay, Christal. I'm tougher than I look."

"Yeah, I know."

Pain lay bright in Sheela's blue eyes. "If you hadn't been there, we'd never have known." A pause. "I wonder, would it have been better that way?"

# CHAPTER 27

The cell phone in Hank's pocket rang twice before he could stumble from the Marriott's bed to the chair where he'd flung his coat the night before. The hotel room had a brownish look in the dim light. Much nicer than the Best Western and without any connection to Marsha. He glanced at the bedside clock: 8:23. Morning, he assumed, and wished he'd been easier on the bourbon last night.

"Yeah?"

*"Abrams? That you?"*

He recognized the voice. "Hey, Larry. What's happening in New York these days?"

*"Just the usual. Lot of tension out there since COVID killed the commercial real estate market. Too many bankruptcies. We've got half the population under surveillance. Kidnapping is up; drugs are down. I'm up to my ass in paperwork, and I've got a hot date with a grand jury on Friday. Which is why I'm in the office today. I got your voice mail."*

"And?"

*"Sure, we know about Verele Security. We work with them a lot. They're on the up-and-up. It's an international executive security firm. Big time. They specialize in high-profile personages. They had someone in our office last week. Some Saudi prince was in town for a bunch of medical procedures. Hush, hush, very sensitive. Maybe the guy had VD and didn't want the local mullahs back home to know. You get the picture?"*

"Anything suspicious about them? You hear any rumors?"

*"Nope. Why, you got something I should know for a heads-up?"*

"Nah, it's just that, well, they've offered me a job. Sort of. If I pass the test."

*"All I can tell you is that from our end, our dealings with them have been professional all the way. Especially with the ebbing and flowing of the terrorist threat. Like I say, they do a lot of Arab leaders, rich Asian businessmen, and that sort of thing. Mostly they try to keep their clients, and their clients' security, from rubbing with the public. Sometimes it's tied up with diplomatic stuff at the UN, and sometimes it's exiled leaders here for different reasons. If you got right down to it, I'm sure you'd find that some of their clientele are scum, but that just comes with the territory."* A pause. *"You going to do this?"*

"I don't know. Larry, I'll level. I got my balls busted. Demotion and transfer to El Paso. Political, if you get my drift. The assistant director himself recommended Verele Security."

*"Shit happens,"* Larry said neutrally. *"They've got an office in the city. Flatiron Building, I think."*

"Yeah." Hank looked down at his knees; his bare feet were kneading the carpet. "Listen, if they schedule an interview, how'd you like to do lunch? Or would you be seen in public with a pariah like me?"

*"Call when you get here."*

# CHAPTER 28

Lymon placed a hand on his unruly stomach. How many years had it been since he had had butterflies like this? Five at least since that last mission into Iran. It had been his final HELO—high-elevation, low-opening parachute drop—into a hostile environment. Naval intelligence needed positive identification of a chemical plant since the Iranians had built it in the middle of a residential area—and next door to an orphanage for good measure.

Lymon and his team had used a handheld laser targeting device to ensure that the navy jets hammered exactly the right building from exactly the right direction. They even had to dope the wind so that it carried the fumes away from the kids.

He felt the butterflies again as he walked down the hall, past the Southwestern art, and stopped at Sheela's door. He tapped lightly at the carved wood.

"Come," came the tired response.

Lymon opened the door, entered the parlor, and found Sheela curled on one of the chaise lounges.

Across from her, the giant TV displayed Russell Crowe in *Gladiator*. He was enthusiastically slicing, dicing, and lopping off limbs. Since the sound was off, it looked curiously surreal. Sheela, however, might have been oblivious as she stared vacantly into the corner. A half-empty cup of tea perched on a silver platter to her right.

"You asked for me?" He walked over and sat on the overstuffed couch across from her.

"Rex just left."

"I know. He sent me up."

"He thinks I should can you."

"If you would be more comfortable that way, I understand."

She looked up with distaste. "Lymon, shut up!"

He lifted an eyebrow at the tone in her voice.

A faint smile appeared, then died at the comers of her mouth. "I need you too much right now."

"We haven't been doing such a hot job. First New York, then last night"

"That's not why I need you." A pause. "Well, yes, there's that too."

"Christal reamed me pretty good. She was wondering just why, exactly, I only had male security guys to keep track of a female principal." He paused. "She did a good job last night, didn't she?"

Sheela raised her eyes. "How's she feeling?"

"Sore. She showed me the bruises. Whatever Copperhead hit her with, I'm surprised she could go running in pursuit."

"Just a fist." Sheela shook her head. "I saw it. Saw Christal's expression as that woman slugged her in the gut. It had to hurt. Is she still blaming herself?"

"Yeah. Like me, she seems to take these things personally."

Sheela seemed to fade. "You don't know what personal is. It's all over the papers."

"I know. Dot slammed an assortment of today's editions on the conference table. The slug lines were creative, to say the least."

Sheela's lips trembled. "Do you know how *creepy* it is? They maneuvered me right into that stall, lined it with plastic, and stole my...my—" Her eyes were imploring. "Who'd steal a woman's *tampon,* for God's sake? How sick can you get?"

"Well, do you want me to think about it for a while? I've got a wild and very creative imagination."

The attempt at humor succeeded in getting nothing more than another quiver of her lips.

Sheela took a deep breath, sighed, and slapped hands onto her knees. "Hell, I should know better. It's just the price you pay in this business."

"It must feel like being raped."

"Believe me, it's very different." She fixed him with a steady stare. "Why, Lymon, I've taken you by surprise! A woman who takes risks—like I always have —gets slapped down by life on occasion."

"On occasion?"

"The first time was in Saskatoon that time I ran away. One night, under a bridge." She looked away, as if evaluating her past. "A great many things happened as a result of that forbidden motorcycle, didn't they?"

"I'm sorry. I'd change it for you if I could."

"I wouldn't let you. I wouldn't be who I am today but for those events." She turned her eyes to his, watching for some sign. "Does it bother you? Knowing that I've been raped?"

He leaned forward, bracing his elbows on his knees. "I'd be a dirty liar if I said no and shrugged it off. But the past is the past. You are who you are, and that's who I've come to regard and respect."

"Regard and respect?" she asked dryly. "My, I would have needed rubbing alcohol to say it with greater sterility."

She paused. "What would you say if I asked you to stay with me tonight?"

He could see the desperation in her eyes. "Sure. I'll set up camp out here. You've got a great library."

"What if I wanted you in there?" She indicated the closed double doors that led to her bedroom.

"I'd have to decline unless I could bring someone, maybe Christal, with me."

Her chuckle was humorless. "Ah, Lymon, always professional. It's okay. I won't ask you. Won't compromise your professional ethics."

"Look, Sheela, you're upset, off balance, and desperate to find some kind of stability. You don't want me. I'm not the man you think I am. Trust me on this, huh?"

She reached out for her tea. "Did you know there are people who make a hobby of memorizing the names of actors who have committed suicide and overdosed? Is that macabre, or what?"

"Why bring that up?"

"Because I finally understand way down in my bones why they do it. Not the people who keep count, but the suicides." She sipped her tea, looking down into the brown liquid. "It caught me right out of left field, the biggest surprise of all."

"What's that?"

"I never anticipated the incredible loneliness that comes with success. They're all standing in line, thousands of them, all wanting something from Sheela Marks. Since the Oscar, they've been hammering down Rex's door. It seems like the entire world wants me to give, but I, on the other hand, can't even share my only friend's company for a night."

"I'm not your only friend."

"Aren't you? Who else will give me a motorcycle ride? Do you have *any* idea how precious that day was to me? Damn, Lymon, for those few marvelous hours we were free, you and me. I was just a woman, and you were just a man, and we were having fun."

"It was fun."

"When I'm harried, frustrated, scared, or angry, I take that memory out and play it from start to finish. From the moment you walked out by the pool, to the expression on your face when I came out with that helmet, to the gleam in your eyes when we stopped for soda." She paused. "The miracle is that there are people out there who can do that every day if they want."

"All right, some morning, when traffic's light, we'll sneak out and do it again."

"I want a life to go with my career, Lymon."

"Hey, that's pushing your luck."

"Yeah, well, instead of a life, I've got people humiliating me for all the world to see. Why would they take a tampon? It was soaked in urine. Hell, for that matter, how could they know I was having my period? Jeez, what are these people? Psychic freaks?"

"As far as I can tell, yeah. Look, we've got the whole team spread around the house. Paul is spelling John on the security cameras. The press is driving past in a constant caravan since the police have a patrol car parked out front to keep them moving. You're as secure as you can get short of pillboxes, sandbags, and a minefield."

"I'm feeling alone and violated, Lymon." She stared at him with weary eyes. "Cut me a deal. Just stay with me. You sit there. I'll sit here. We'll talk. About anything and everything. Watch movies all night...read books. Hell, I don't care. Call for coffee every thirty minutes so that you know that the staff knows that you're being professional. Whatever you feel comfortable with." Her control began to collapse. *"Is that too much to ask?"*

# CHAPTER 29

C hristal blinked and glared at the screen on her MacBook. She was sitting on an uncomfortable chair at the kitchen table in her Residence Inn suite. After too many hours of bright Internet screens, a person started having visions. Her *curandera* grandmother would have approved. The effect was something akin to peyote but without the bitter taste and having to repeatedly throw up.

She yawned, shifting to get blood back into her butt. When she reached for her coffee cup, the last swallow was cold and bitter. Stains had dried around the rim, and rings marked the interior. How many hours had she been here, working so hard to find nothing?

The news stories abounded with accounts of the curious theft of Sheela's tampon. The press was titillated and the tabloids ecstatic. Public commentary was sporadic and, so far, found only in editorials. A lot of celebrity memorabilia was for sale on eBay and the other sites, but no one offered a used Sheela Marks' tampon.

Having exhausted everything else, she went back to Sheela's Web site and monitored the chat rooms. There, too, she found lots of conversations asking why their idol had been so publicly scorched. Christal monitored a couple of people who wished they could emulate the deed and wrote down their addresses.

In the end, she found herself back at the main menu, staring mindlessly at the screen. On impulse, she linked to Genesis Athena and inspected their questionnaire. What was her name, her age, her sex? Was Sheela Marks her favorite actor? How many times a week did she watch Sheela Marks? How many times a month? What was her salary? Her net financial worth? State her highest educational level. Had she ever written a fan letter? What were her views on adoption? On government regulation of biotech firms? Did she fear traveling abroad? And so forth.

She was tired of questions—most notably of the question, "Why?"

Signing off, she stood and arched her back, trying to get the kinks out. The refrigerator hummed, and the TV in the living room flashed images from the news, the sound barely audible.

A vigorous knock came at her door.

"Lymon, if that's you, I'm going to kill you." She glanced at her watch. He might be paying her very well, but she'd been up all the previous night. That morning she'd done a turn with the LAPD forensic artist before returning to her apartment, where she'd spent five hours on the computer looking for clues. She had to sleep sometime.

At the peephole, she was surprised to see Rex Gerber standing with his hands in his expensive trouser pockets. Sunlight was shining on the scalp beneath his thinning black hair. His eyes were gleaming behind his fleshy nose. A tan jacket covered a light-blue shirt.

"Good afternoon, Mr. Gerber," she said as she opened the door. "What's wrong?"

"Wrong? Nothing." He gave her a quizzical look as he stepped in. "You feeling okay?"

She nodded, leading him into the small living room. "Let me guess, my eyes look like Pennsylvania road maps, and I could bring groceries home in the bags under my eyes."

He looked around. "This is nice. I've never been in one before. Kitchen, couch, all the comforts of home."

"Have a seat. What can I do for you?"

Rex flopped back in the couch and bounced, evidently trying it out for comfort. Then he turned his attention to Christal. "I thought maybe we'd go out for a drink."

"Let me rain check. It's been too long since I caught a full eight hours. Lymon didn't let me off the night patrol until well after sunup. And then the day really started."

"So, what have you been doing?"

She indicated the computer at the kitchen table. "Research that had to be done immediately. I've been all over the internet." She settled on the arm of the chair across from him. "If someone was making a point, something should have cropped up somewhere. Every search I've run has come up empty."

His fleshy face screwed up. "You kidding? It's the talk of the town. My people have worn calluses on their ears answering the phones and calluses on their fingers from texting. Everyone wants to know what's going on."

"Oh, yeah, I found a lot of talk, Mr. Gerber. Lots of discussion of who, why, and what's next, but nothing from anybody who's saying, 'I got it! What am I bid?'"

He frowned. "I haven't mentioned this to Sheela, but the gals that did this might be totally bent and kinky, you know? Golden showers with Sheela's piss? And the tampon? What? Paint themselves? Flagellation? I don't wanna shock you, but sometimes people get really sick."

Christal clasped her hands together. "I suspect, Mr. Gerber, that I know more about deviant criminal behavior than you do. We have entire courses at the Bureau dedicated to it, but I don't think so. Not this time."

"Why not?"

"It's the second try at Sheela. The guy in New York didn't get the job done."

"Come on, that was clear across the country. He was a guy. This was two girls. You're saying there's three of them?"

"At least. Maybe more when you factor in the other celeb hits. All of them are taking something really personal. Sheets and toothbrushes, razor scuzz, and tampons are all shockingly intimate. And with at least three people involved, and striking from here to Australia, it's not just kinky sexual behavior."

"So what is it?"

"Mr. Gerber, I can't tell you yet. But it's going to be something really sensational."

"You know, I've been in this business for a long

time. The lengths that some people will go to is astounding. There was a guy once who had himself shipped to one of my client's houses. Had himself nailed into a crate and delivered. Can you imagine? All that just so he could get inside the house. Turns out the client was in England shooting a picture. The household staff got curious when the box started to smell like piss and shit, so they opened it. Good thing, too—the guy was half-dead from dehydration."

"Some people live for their obsessions, Mr. Gerber."

He gave her a penetrating look. "Can we get past this Mr. Gerber thing?"

Weary as she was, it took a moment to comprehend the interest in his brown eyes. *Crap. So that's why he's here.*

"Sure, Rex. Look, I'm sorry to be a spoilsport, but I've got to kick you out and get some shut-eye."

He hadn't moved, deporting himself as an alpha male, with his arm thrown back on the couch. "Yeah, Lymon's a slave driver."

"Scuttlebutt says you wanted Sheela to fire him."

He shrugged. "Someone got to my client. What can I say? I overreact sometimes. I know Lymon's the best, but I really care about Sheela. If it hadn't been for you, we'd have never known she'd even been tapped." He was giving her "the look" again.

"Come on," she told him as she stood. "Up and at 'em. I'll have that drink with you, but only after I figure this thing out."

He smiled, then eased onto his feet. "You know, I like you, Christal. You've got chops. I think you're going to go far in this business."

She smiled as she opened the door, a big hint that

he was sharp enough to get. "I haven't proven myself yet."

"You have to me." He gave her a broad smile. "I'll be seeing you later."

"Good night, Rex."

"Yeah, you get some sleep, huh?"

She closed the door and slumped against it. Men. He had to have twenty-five years on her. He was older than her father would have been.

"Christ," she muttered as she locked the door.

# CHAPTER 30

Sid Harness searched the crowd as he cleared LAX security. A throng of people were waiting, some waving as they joined the effluvium of arriving passengers on their way to the baggage claim.

"Sid!" He heard Christal's voice at the same time he saw her wave. His bag in one hand, his coat over his arm, he could only nod and smile as she worked through the press.

God, she looked good. He could see the fatigue around her eyes, but her posture was straight. Her hair was done up in an attractive style. Time had tricked his imagination; she looked better than he remembered. Even a little tanned.

"Hey, Christal!" He gave her a partial hug, as much as his bag would allow. "So, how's LA?"

She laughed as she stepped in beside him. "I'm sick. In need of psychological counseling."

"Why's that?"

"Because I love it here. Oh, not the traffic and the crowds, but hey, that's a city anywhere, huh?"

"Yep." He glanced at her. "You're looking happy, Chris. I can't tell you how glad that makes me."

"Thanks to you. 'Fall on your sword,' you said. 'There's life after death.' So, yeah, I'm alive. But, by God, I'm going to get you for saddling me with that workaholic son of a bitch."

"That's my old buddy, Lymon, you're talking about."

She gave him a wry smile. "I gotta tell you, this private sector is a ball buster. Unlike the Bureau, when I mention overtime, Lymon just raises an eyebrow and asks, 'How much are we paying you?'"

Sid grinned, waving her off when she pointed questioningly at the baggage carousel. "I've got everything in the bag. Where are your wheels?"

"This way. I'm in short term. It's a bit of a walk. I couldn't get Lymon's fancy Escalade with the park-for-free-anywhere permit." She led the way out through the doors and across the pedestrian crossing. "How long are you in town?"

"Three days. I booked early so we could have some time. First thing tomorrow I'm due in the LA Field Office. Unless something comes up, I'm out of here at oh-dark-thirty Wednesday morning."

"Where are you staying?"

"After tonight, I'm at the Hotel El-Cheapo just down the street from the FO. I've got the address here someplace. Lymon talked me into bunking with him tonight. Said he'd drop me off downtown *mañana*."

"You've known him a long time?"

"Yeah. *Semper fi*." He smiled. "I owe the guy my life."

"What was he like back then? Intense?"

"That's a mild word for it." Sid glanced at her. "He had one speed: full throttle. And that last year, he was headed straight for the proverbial brick wall." He paused. "So, tell me. What about it? Did I do right sending you here?"

She gave him that sloe-eyed glance that always teased his masculinity. "Yeah, Sid. I think. To tell you the truth, I've been running from the moment I got here." She paused. "As to Lymon, well, he's different. Right now he's got us all pushing. I'm supposed to be tracking down Sheela Marks' assailants, but I'm spending half my time at the principal's. She's a little freaked at having her personal waste lifted."

"I heard you took a couple of belts to the gut."

Her lip lifted, eyes hardening. "It won't happen again."

"I gotta know, what's Sheela Marks really like?"

"She's a lot like the roles she plays in her films. Tough and vulnerable. I'm worried about her."

"Why?"

"She's living in a pressure cooker. What happened on Friday doesn't help. I think she'd like to take a week off to indulge in a nice emotional breakdown. Her manager won't schedule it for her."

"She's got a manager?"

"You bet. A real zirconium jewel. He wants to take me out for a drink and dinner. You know, get acquainted before he adds me to his list of conquests."

"Yeah?"

"He's in his fifties. And kind of an asshole. I've got better taste than that." She looked suddenly chastened. "Or, maybe, come to think of it, I don't, huh?"

After she took a breath, she asked, "So, speaking of

asholes, how's Hank doing? Happy in his new assignment?"

"He's gone."

"What?"

"Resigned." Sid chuckled. "Would you believe it? He's working for an outfit called Verele Security out of New York. Who knows, you two might bump into each other on some movie set somewhere."

"That ought to be interesting. Do you think our clients will have the sense to get out of the way while I try to cut his balls off?"

"Marsha filed for divorce. Someone—probably Gonzales—sent her the photos. On top of that, Hank got dropped a pay grade and was being reassigned to El Paso."

"I like El Paso."

"Of course you'd like El Paso. You're from New Mexico. He's from Massachusetts."

"So, am I to assume he's coming here?"

"Nope. New York last I heard."

Sid did a double-take when she stopped at a slick new Tahoe. "This is your ride?"

"It's just a rental. Job perk, you know?"

"I'm in the wrong business." He slid into the passenger seat, watching Christal out of the corner of his eye as she backed out, drove to the exit, and handed the ticket to the attendant. As they followed the signs to the 405, he added, "I haven't seen you look this happy in a long time, Chris."

She ran slim fingers through her thick black hair. "I don't know why. Twenty-hour days can't be good for me." Then she flashed him a sexy grin and her eyes sparkled. "But, yeah, I'm having the time of my life. How about you?"

"Screwed," he muttered. "This abduction thing, if it is an abduction, is driving me nuts."

"So, tell me."

"What's to tell? I've got a graduate student—female —from over in Georgetown who just drops off the face of the earth. One day she's there, about to defend her doctoral dissertation on manipulating phases of the cell cycle. What do I know about cell cycles? Hell, if a cell has a cycle, I assume it's a Suzuki, right?"

"What do you mean, 'dropped off the face of the earth'?"

"I mean, zero. *Nada*. She leaves her lab to go for a job interview with a biotech firm and never makes the appointment. She's gone. Keyser Soze gone."

"So why are you involved? It's a missing persons report; you don't have probable cause to make a kidnapping determination. Fifty-fifty says she got burned out and skipped, willing to give up the pressure-cooker bullshit of a PhD program in return for sitting on a beach somewhere selling T-shirts."

"Yeah, maybe." He used the buttons to adjust the seat back. "Thing is, there's a pattern of this. Goes back five years. Over that time, no less than twenty-two hotshot young geneticists have vanished. Risen like smoke and drifted away. In each case, there hasn't been a thing. Nothing. Not a body, not a ransom note. No sightings by acquaintances."

He chewed at his lip. "Then, last Friday, just before you did the tango with that menstrual thief, a white male, Mike Harris, age twenty-four, leaves the UCLA genetics lab to take a whiz. What should have been a three-minute bladder tapping has stretched into almost seventy-two hours now."

"Yeah, well a word of warning: You gotta watch out in these LA bathrooms."

He smiled. "Seriously, what do you think?"

"Seventy-two hours? That's a long time for a man to pee, and he's way too young for prostate problems."

# CHAPTER 31

The place was called Al's. Lymon had stumbled across it several years ago. The atmosphere was nice with walls paneled in dark wood, and classical folk music played on the speakers. Not only that, Al had a deal with some Wyoming buffalo ranchers. He got a frozen package twice a week. Al's jalapeno-cheddar buffalo burgers were handmade, cooked to perfection, and melted in the mouth. He also made what he called "Sioux soup," which was buffalo meat, sunflower seeds, pumpkin seeds, squash, potatoes, blue corn flour, pinon nuts, and Anasazi beans. In addition to ancho chili powder, he used fresh poblano peppers and cilantro. It could knock your socks off.

Lymon leaned back in the barrel-shaped chair and grinned at Sid as he finished his burger and washed it down with a glass of Stone Porter. "Not bad, huh?"

"I could live like this." Sid made a face. "Those jalapenos, though, whew!"

"Homegrown." Lymon copped a glance at Christal. There were advantages to being raised New Mexican.

You didn't break a sweat over something as innocuous as garden-raised peppers.

"So," Christal asked, "do the guys on the squad still hiss when they speak my name?"

"Yeah. Some. Everybody's pissed because Gonzales got away." He paused. "The son of a bitch knows just how close we came to busting his ass. That's worth something."

Christal's eyes had clouded as she stared at her plate. She'd eaten a tender buffalo steak, medium rare. "If we can link him to the celebrity heists, we'll give you the goods on him."

"He's not into Michael Jordan's jockstrap, thank you." Sid wiped his lips with the napkin and sipped more beer. He glanced at Christal. "You've got a nose for these things. What do you think? Trophies?"

Christal shook her head. "It's not right. Trophies suggest a victory. Taking something as a hard-won memento. If that's the case, what's the contest? Just breaking security? Why not take Roberts' Oscar, or Gibson's whole razor? Trophy taking, by its very nature, is the removal of something the target values. It indicates assertive-oriented behavior."

"So," Sid countered, "if it's not trophies, it's souvenirs."

Christal gave him a censorial glare. "You never were much for criminal psychology, Sid. Souvenirs are generally linked to reassurance-oriented behavior. The woman I dealt with in the ladies' john at the Wilshire didn't need much in the way of reassurance. Trust me on that. My abs are still tender to the touch."

"Really?" Sid gave her an animated grin. "Can I feel?"

"I thought you had to be on a plane in three days." She gave him a look that would have warped titanium. "You'll be that long just getting out of intensive care."

"Meanwhile—getting back to the case—are we dealing with a symbolic action?" Lymon asked. "Taking someone's tampon has got to make some kind of point."

"Yeah?" Christal asked. "Symbolic of what? That Sheela Marks—along with most every other woman in the world—has a functioning reproductive tract?"

"At least you know she's not pregnant," Sid mused.

"We weren't worried about that," Lymon answered. "And if you assume these things are related, I don't think Mel Gibson was, either."

"If that's the case, there are way too many people for a sociopath to be involved." Sid fingered his beer glass.

"Unless it's a rich sociopath." Christal was staring into the distance. "Sid, I've just started to understand the things someone with money can do. If you pay enough, you can hire anyone to do anything. I mean, damn, how much does it take to get a camera into an FBI surveillance van? What's a tampon and some urine compared to that?"

Sid shook his head. "I don't know. Does stealing the kind of stuff we're talking about fit into any of the standard typologies?"

"It's definitely one hell of an invasion of privacy." Lymon pushed his empty bowl back and placed the spoon in it. With a lifted finger to the waiter, he indicated that the plates needed busing.

"Another round," Sid said as the man picked up the dishes.

Lymon noticed that Christal was on her second Sierra Nevada Pale Ale. "I'd started to come to the conclusion that she didn't drink. Sid, you're a good influence."

"Who? Chris? When she gets wound up, you need a funnel with a tube just to keep up with her."

"I don't do that anymore." Christal had lowered her eyes. Was that an embarrassed flush at her throat?

Sid shrugged. "No, I guess you don't."

"Want to fill me in?" Lymon asked gently.

"It was just a joke," Sid said bluffly. Hell, he didn't lie any better now than he did in the Corps.

Christal turned her dark eyes to his. "The last time I had too much, I crawled into a surveillance van. Just me and my AIC."

"You don't have to do this," Sid said gently.

"Nope." Lymon sensed her discomfort.

Christal shrugged, fingering her beer. "It's all right. I made a mistake. Would I have made the mistake if I'd been stone-cold sober? I don't know. Maybe. Probably. I liked the guy."

"He was scuzz," Sid muttered and gave Lymon a meaningful glance. "I don't get it. The guy's a dickhead, but women always fawn over him."

"It was his eyes," Christal told them. "The way he smiled. How he listened."

She gave Sid a disapproving look. "It's a trick you might want to learn. When Hank is listening to a woman, he pays complete attention to her. He treats her like at that moment she is the single most important thing in his world."

"So? I listen to women."

"Yeah, Sid. With half an ear."

"But the guy was gutless!" Sid ended with a snort of derision as the waiter laid down another round.

Christal shrugged. "We didn't know that until the shit hit the fan. When it did, he took it like a whipped puppy."

Sid poured rich dark porter into his glass, studied the brown head, and said, "I think his time with Marsha was running out anyway. She was married to him. She knew what a loser he was. Flashy, with no guts. I'd bet he was whining when she threw him out."

"Whining is underrated," Lymon offered. "I whine a lot. It helps me get my way."

In the middle of a swallow, Sid laughed—and almost puked as he coughed and pawed for a napkin.

"You whine?" Christal asked. "Can I watch next time?"

"Sure. I think I have a whining session scheduled for next week. Check with June. She does the calendar."

Sid coughed again, belched, and placed a hand to his stomach. "Excuse me. Damn. You shouldn't do that, Lymon. Not when I'm vulnerable."

"You're always vulnerable. Speaking of which, when are you going to get off the government dole and come work with us real professionals?"

"If you're going to tempt a federal employee," Christal said, rising, "I'm off to the ladies' room."

"Keep an eye out for Copperhead," Lymon called.

Christal shot a look over her shoulder. "I hope she's there. She and I have this little thing that we need to settle."

They watched her walk to the hallway in the rear.

"Damn, that's a nice sight," Sid said with a sigh. "I really miss having her around. Not only is she just a good kid, but I used to spend half the day dreaming about that body."

Lymon chuckled. "You're married."

"So? I can still dream, can't I?" Sid refolded his napkin. "Okay, yeah, I guess I fell a little in love with Christal. Who wouldn't?"

"Hank?"

"Shit! But for him, she'd have had a dynamite career." Sid shook his head. "Weird thing. You and I both know it's not the first time a male and female agent made whoopee on surveillance; they just didn't do it when the target was Gonzales. We're still trying to figure out how the hell he got a camera into that van."

"Someone in the Bureau?"

"Probably." Sid looked up. "If Gonzales found out that Hank Abrams was in charge of the investigation, it wouldn't have taken him long to figure out just what kind of guy he was. Half the WMFO knew he was screwing around on Marsha." He made a face. "Fucking pretty boy."

"So why don't you ditch the bullshit? I could use a partner."

"Me? A partner?"

Lymon made a gesture of surrender. "Well, maybe. We'd have to see if June would hire you."

"That's the secretary?"

"Business manager."

"Right." Sid paused and jerked his head toward the women's room. "So, how's she doing?"

"Good. You steered me right. If she likes the work, I'd like to keep her."

Sid seemed fascinated by a spot on the tablecloth when he said, "You thought about asking her out?"

Lymon gave him the evil eye when he finally looked up. "Is that why you sent her out here?"

"You seen a more beautiful woman recently?"

"I work for Sheela Marks." Lymon grinned at Sid's sudden discomfort and added, "I only owe you my life and my soul. Don't try to play matchmaker for me."

Christal returned a moment later and dropped into the chair with an easy grace. "So, did you guys get an angle on the celeb bits while I was gone, or did you spend the whole time talking about me?"

"Talked about you," Lymon said blandly. "You're a lot more interesting."

Sid had recovered completely, saying, "Well, if it's not profit motivated, it's payback, right?"

Lymon made a helpless gesture. "Sheela's never done a movie with any of those people."

"Any personal relationship with any of them?" Christal asked.

"Well, sure, there's the professional similarity, but that's about it. Are there mutual friends? You bet. It's the film business. Everybody knows everybody."

Sid leaned forward. "Maybe it's someone who got stepped on. An actor who lost a key role to Marks, or one of the others? Maybe it's something simple like they were repped by the same agency or something?"

Christal shrugged. "I can start checking on that." Her expression dropped. "One thing about the Bureau. You can always get people to do the scut work."

Sid cocked an eyebrow, lowering his voice. "So, Lymon. Assuming you find this guy, what are you going to do about him?"

Lymon tried to keep his voice calm when he said, "Paybacks are a bitch, aren't they?"

Christal was watching him, hearing more than he wanted to say. He tried to decipher the look she was giving him. Definitely evaluative.

"Be very, *very* careful, old friend." No levity could be heard in Sid's voice.

# CHAPTER 32

Sheela Marks' filmography on Wikipedia consisted of no less than thirty-three titles, and it didn't take Christal long to figure out that this research, like so much that she had done as a federal agent, was tedious, long, and monotonous. Having the dates when the films were made was just the beginning. From there, she went to *Daily Variety,* flipping through the editions looking for Sheela Marks' name. Then she painstakingly had to figure out who was in or out of the deals. After eight hours, she had a list of several hundred names and that was just the actors. Including directors, she could add another fifty. Factor in another twenty-two when the producers were included.

She considered her list, tapped her pen, and glared at the stack of weeklies as she considered having to repeat the effort for each of the other names.

"Ma'am?" the librarian asked as she walked up to the carrel. "Are you about finished? We're closing in fifteen minutes."

"Yes. Thank you." Christal stood, feeling the ache in her back, and began collecting her things. "I'll see you in the morning."

Several names were rubbing against her thoughts as she stepped out into the tawny light of an LA sunset. One of them was Manuel de Clerk.

She pulled out her cell, dialed the office, and got the answering machine as it identified the company and stated the normal operating hours for Lymon Bridges Associates. June, it appeared, got to keep a normal human being's work hours.

Christal called Lymon.

On the second ring, he answered, *"Bridges."*

"Lymon? Anaya. I'm looking for Tony Zell's number."

*"Agency or personal?"*

"How do I get a hold of him tonight?"

*"Got a pen?"*

"Ten-four."

She scribbled the number he gave her on the corner of her legal pad where it stuck out of her purse. "Thanks, Lymon."

*"Business or pleasure?"*

"You're a funny man, boss. A stitch a minute. When would I have time for pleasure?"

*"So, what have you got?"*

"Did you know that Sheela Marks got Manuel de Clerk bounced from *Blood Rage?* The guy was supposed to play the lead. Sheela insisted they find someone else."

*"Yeah."*

"She got him chopped out of a real juicy role."

*"And you're thinking Manny's been holding a grudge?"*

"I want to talk to the guy. I figure Tony can open the door for me. Does he represent de Clerk?"

*"Nope. But he knows who does. Give Tony a call. Keep me informed."*

"Right."

*"Christal?"*

"Yeah?"

*"About de Clerk. Do me a favor. Be discreet, huh? Don't piss the guy off. It would really upset my digestion if his lawyer started baying outside of my bedroom window over some silly slander suit."*

"Gotcha, boss."

She killed the call and tapped in Tony's number.

He answered on the third ring. Music was blaring in the background. *"This is Tony."*

"Mr. Zell? I don't know if you remember me. I'm Christal Anaya, working for—"

*"Cool! Christal! Hey, I've been thinking about you. You know, you promised me dinner, babe."*

She made a face. Babe? "I was hoping you could direct me to Manuel de Clerk. I need to speak with him concerning the events at the Beverly Wilshire the other night. Nothing important, just some questions. Strictly business for LBA."

*"Yeah. Glad to help. It'll cost you, though."*

"How's that?" she asked coolly.

He broke into hysterical laughter. *"Hey, Christal, you're too far out there! Chill, babe. I don't need a bribe—at least not like that. Dinner. Tomorrow. Eight thirty. You say yeah, I give you the number of Manny's digs and a phone call to let him know you're coming. Cool?"*

"Cool."

*"Fucking A! And don't forget, you already said yeah at*

*the reception just before you hammered that bitch that tried to snag Sheela."*

"I did?" Maybe he didn't remember who hammered whom?

*"Hey, I shoulda got it on tape, huh?"*

"I guess so."

*"Right! What's your number? Let me make a few calls. Maybe Manny can see you tonight. Just professional, huh? Don't make me jealous!"*

She lifted her lip but said in a sweet voice, "I wouldn't think of it."

She hung up and waited. Within five minutes, her phone rang.

*"Hey ya, Christal? Tony here. I got it worked out."*

"Okay. What, when, and where?"

*"His digs, babe. Nine o'clock tonight. Ring one long, two short and one long. The gate will open. He'll be at the big house."*

"Thank you, Mr. Zell."

*"Hey, babe. It's Tony. No sweat. Dinner tomorrow, right?"*

# CHAPTER 33

Lymon's garage was a three-car affair. In one bay, he kept a gray Toyota Land Cruiser, in the next his personal car, a Jaguar F Type, and finally his motorcycles. In the rear, a pristine 1975 Moto Guzzi California Highway Patrol model rested on its center stand, the chrome fenders gleaming. His BMW stood closest to the door, the bodywork removed, the rocker boxes off to expose the oil-slicked valve assemblies. Finally, a red-and-bronze 2003 Indian Chief Deluxe canted on its side stand, the thick fenders polished and shining. The leather saddle had a waxed look, and chromed diamonds glinted in the skirt. Two fringed leather saddlebags hung low at the rear.

A radio on a shelf in the back was set on KABC to make white noise as Lymon worked on the BMW. His red toolbox was open, several of the drawers at half-jut. He sat on an inverted bucket and used an Allen wrench to turn the BMW's crank to top dead center. Air sucked and puffed from the empty spark-plug holes as the valve springs compressed and then released. Lymon glanced in the inspection hole for the timing mark. As his fingers wiggled the rocker arms, he rolled the events of the last two weeks around inside his head. The thing that stuck with him was the look of terror in Sheela's eyes, the pulsing of the vein in her neck after the attack at the St. Regis. That was followed by her abject humiliation at the Wilshire. What in hell could he have done differently?

The soft whisper of an engine and the rasping of tires intruded. He looked up, seeing the long black nose of the limo rounding the curve of his drive and pulling to a stop.

He stood, grabbing a red rag and wiping his hands as he walked to the open door. Paul was giving him a worried look when he opened the driver's door and started around the front of the long vehicle.

"Paul? What the hell are you..." Lymon stopped short when the rear door opened, and Sheela climbed out. She was carrying a canvas duffel bag in one hand, her purse hanging from her shoulder.

"He's doing what he's supposed to," she called, striding toward him. "Thank you, Paul. Please take the car home. Lymon can bring me when I'm finished."

"Hey," Lymon protested. "Sheela, are you nuts?"

She made a shooing gesture. "Bye, Paul. And thank you."

Paul looked back and forth, confused, and muttered, "Yes, ma'am," before walking back and slipping into the driver's seat. He put the long black car into reverse and backed slowly around the curve of the drive.

"This is my home," Lymon protested. "Sheela, what are you doing here?"

She was dressed in form-fitting jeans that hugged her toned hips and long legs. Thick-soled black boots covered her feet. A gray long-sleeved blouse was tucked into her pants and did little to disguise her famous bustline. She had her red-gold hair in the French braid again. Wary blue eyes met his as she stepped past, frowning at the BMW with its sundry pieces scattered around the cement floor.

"What's wrong with your Beemer?"

"Nothing. It's just that you have to set the valve clearance every six thousand miles. While I was at it, I changed the oil. That's in that pan over there. I was just setting the intake side."

"So, it's not really broken."

"What are you doing here?"

She took a deep breath and turned. "I'm escaping, Lymon."

The look she gave him melted his heart and over-whelmed his good sense. "Okay. So, you've escaped." He chuckled, wiping his hands. "Now what?"

She made a halfhearted gesture toward the disas-sembled RT. "Well, I was thinking of another soda up at that place on the other side of the Angeles Crest." She turned, frowning at the Indian. "What about that one?"

He glanced at the canvas war bag in her hand. "Let me guess, that's the helmet and leather jacket, right?"

She gave him a conspiratorial smile. "Could you do it for me, Lymon? Set me free again for a couple of hours?"

"It's not smart, you know."

She stepped closer to him, a desperate soul behind her searching blue eyes. "Hell, I know that. It's prob-ably going to end in a wreck one way or another. But

God, if I don't do something, I'm going to lose my mind."

"Yeah, well, when you get into trouble, it seems like there's always a motorcycle at the bottom of it." He indicated the sleek steel-blue Jaguar. "Sure you wouldn't rather save my heart a little wear and tear and take the Jag?"

She bent, unzipping the bag to pull out her helmet. "If I'm headed to hell, Lymon, I say go all the way."

"Can I at least finish the valves?"

His heart skipped at the joy reflected in her smile. "Sure. I can even help." She held up her long delicate fingers, manicured to perfection. "You'd be surprised. These have actually been oil-stained. And I helped rebuild the injectors on a Massey Ferguson once."

"I'm all atwitter." Lymon smiled and returned to his bucket. God, this wasn't smart. But when he looked at Sheela, glowing with relief as she bent down to help him with the lock nuts and feeler gauges, he couldn't help himself.

*Shit. I'm completely, totally, helplessly in love with her.* "Just like every other red-blooded male in the world."

"What was that?" Sheela was sorting through the feeler gauges like dealing cards.

"Nothing that couldn't be cured by a bullet to the brain."

# CHAPTER 34

As evening fell, Christal wound her Tahoe through Brentwood's curving streets and slowed before a wooded lot. Behind a high wrought-iron fence and through the trees, she could just glimpse an imposing Tudor-style house. She checked her watch: 8:32.

She pulled up at the curb and slipped the car into park. The last of the sunset's glow was fading in the reddened west. Streetlights were flickering on. Rolling the driver's window down, she could hear insects and distant traffic on the evening air.

So, what was the right strategy? Drive up to the tall, spike-topped gate and ring the buzzer? Or wait until the designated time and act like a real professional?

She wasn't sure what the smart move was yet. This was different than working for the Bureau. Here, she had to operate with people's forbearance.

Her patience wore out at a quarter to nine when she turned the key, brought the Tahoe to life, and drove up to the gate. The metal box perched on a pole on the driver's side had a speaker, camera, and buzzer. She rolled her window down the rest of the way and reached out to ring long, short, short, long.

Like magic, the gate rolled back on its wheels, and Christal drove up the curving lane toward the imposing house. The tree-shrouded drive ended in a loop that surrounded flower gardens and a central cement fountain. Floodlights cast it all in a yellow sodium glow. A Porsche, a stretch Mercedes, and an Audi were parked at the side of the curve in front. The yards were manicured, and the dark grass looked recently mowed.

Christal grabbed her purse and notebook with its list of names and stepped out into the evening. The house lights blazed as she walked up the steps to the door. She was just about to stab the buzzer when a car door opened behind her. She turned, surprised to see a woman stepping out of the Audi's driver's door. She was small-framed, dark-haired, with a narrow face.

"Can I help you?" the woman asked, her voice thin. She was standing with her arms crossed tightly under her small breasts. She wore a white shirt over dark slacks and might have weighed a full one hundred pounds, provided she'd had a big meal and been hosed down.

Christal turned, stepping down the stone stairs. "Yes, I'm here for an appointment with Manuel de Clerk."

"He didn't have an appointment." The woman looked wary, suddenly nervous, tightening her crossed arms. She was squinting, and Christal realized the light was behind her.

"Excuse me, do you work for Mr. de Clerk?" Christal could feel her instincts begin to prickle. In that instant, she knew that face, had seen it when this same mousy-looking woman had stepped out of a toilet stall at the Wilshire but days past.

"Who are you?" Christal's tone sharpened.

The woman's eyes enlarged, and her thin mouth twisted into a faint smile. "I know you." Even as she was speaking, she unfolded her arms and pointed a small silver revolver at Christal's midsection. "Just stand very still."

Christal experienced that electric lightness of the guts as she focused on the dark muzzle of the little snub-nosed revolver. Her skin crawled at the expectation of a bullet.

"Hey," she whispered, trying to get her breath. "Relax. I'm no threat."

"Who are you?" the mousy woman asked, her voice turning shrill.

"I'm Christal Anaya. I work for Sheela Marks." She swallowed hard. Shit, this little short-haired *vaina* wouldn't really shoot her, would she?

"What are you doing here?" Mouse's dark eyes were like stones in her pale face.

"I told you, I've got an appointment with Manuel de Clerk."

"Why?"

"Things for Sheela," she made up. "They're shooting *Jagged Cat*. Look, it's not worth me getting shot over. I'll leave." She took a step back, her arms half-raised.

"You don't move." Mouse held eye contact as she leaned into the Audi, felt about with her other hand, and retrieved something off the dashboard. A little black box that looked like the remote for an automobile's door lock and security system. When Mouse thumbed the button, Christal heard nothing.

Christal made a gesture of surrender. "Look, this isn't my concern. If you're robbing the guy, I don't want any part of it."

Mouse smiled faintly. "Just stand still." She glanced past Christal toward the house, as if expecting someone. Who? Copperhead?

"So, what is it this time?" Christal asked. "I'd almost bet you're not getting a used tampon from Manny."

Mouse's expression reflected amusement, but she said nothing.

"Can I go?" Christal took another step back. "You've made your point."

"I said, don't move."

Christal nodded as she took another step back. Her brain was starting to work again, her training asserting itself. She was a good four steps from the front of her Tahoe. Two steps and a leap and she could be at the door. Did that give her time to pull it open and dive inside?

Was that even a smart option? The silver pistol looked like a .38, but it could just as easily be a .357. Maybe one of the compact Taurus or Smith and Wessons. They were building incredibly powerful pistols into small and lightweight packages. A .357 could make chowder out of auto glass.

*Think!*

She studied the woman, seeing how the tendons stood out on Mouse's hand. She was gripping the pistol like she was squeezing a rubber ball. Christal could see it wiggling in the woman's overstressed grip.

So, what were the odds? Could the woman really shoot? Or was she the kind who had once emptied a box at the range?

*God, what a thing to have to bet on!*

Christal was running options through her head when she heard the door open behind her. She turned, seeing Copperhead as she came striding out of the house. The woman was tucking a blouse into the top of her skirt as her pumps tapped the stone steps. Her familiar purse hung from one shoulder.

"What's the...?" Her eyes fixed on Christal; a momentary puzzlement was replaced by a knowing smile.

"Ah? I know you. I think we're going to have a long chat, you and I."

Mouse had her gaze fixed on Copperhead. Christal bet the farm, spun on her heel, and ran. Feet pounding, arms pumping, she sprinted for the corner of the house, where shadows pooled under a weeping willow.

"Stop her!" Copperhead cried.

Christal couldn't separate the supersonic crack of a bullet from the report of the gun. She jinked right, took two steps, and jinked right again. She lost count of the cracking shots that split the air around her. Then she was in the shadows, darting from side to side. She pitched herself behind the bole of the tree, gasping for breath, heart hammering.

*"What the hell are you doing?"* Copperhead was screaming, her face contorted.

"You said, 'Stop her!'" Mouse cried as she picked at the open cylinder of her gun.

"Damn! We don't need a murder! You stupid little *fool*!"

"She's the same woman from the hotel! She followed us!"

"Come on!" Copperhead cried. "It's too late. The police will be here any second!" She was climbing into the driver's side.

"I think I hit her!" Mouse cried plaintively. "I've got to make sure!" She was slipping bullets into the cylinder, glancing back and forth from the gun to the shadows where Christal hunched behind the willow.

"I'm *leaving!*" Copperhead insisted as the Audi roared to life. "Get in, Gretchen! Or stay here."

Gretchen snapped the cylinder closed, made a face of indecision, and bolted, bracing herself on the moving Audi as she pelted around the rear and sprinted to pull the passenger door open and dive inside.

Christal sagged in the darkness, gasping for breath. Shit! She'd never been shot at before. Bureau training was one thing. It was another to actually have someone try and kill her.

Her hands trembled as she fumbled for her cell phone. The shakes were so bad it took all of her concentration just to punch 911.

*"Emergency response, how can I help you?"* a woman's metallic voice asked.

In the blur of an adrenaline high, Christal sputtered the address, noted that shots had been fired, that the subjects—two females wanted for questioning in regard to an incident at the Wilshire Hotel on Friday—were in a late-model Audi.

*"Is anyone hurt?"* the voice asked.

"My god, Manny!" Christal's legs had gone to rubber. She felt wobbly as she ran for the door. Copperhead had left it swinging wide.

"I'm in the foyer," Christal shouted into the phone. "I'm not touching anything." She raised her voice. "Hello? Is anyone here?"

A voice, faint, could be heard. "Hey! God! Help me!"

Christal ignored the questions the 911 operator was calling and took the carpeted steps two at a time to the top floor. She hurried down the long hall, past doorways that she assumed were bedrooms, to the final door.

"I'm coming!"

"She *cut* me!" the panicked voice cried. "God, cut me loose! *Help me!*"

Christal used her shoulder to push the last door open, taking a good look. She'd found a bedroom, all right. The room was bigger than the entire house she'd grown up in. Expensive white carpeting covered the floor. Most of the walls were mirrored, adding to the illusion of endless space. A huge walk-in closet opened off one side. The master bed was monstrous: a four-poster with a flat wooden canopy that looked like it was carved walnut. She could see the man, naked, spread-eagled. His head was up, the tendons straining in his gleaming neck, and he was staring at his crotch.

Christal's work at crime scenes caused her to pause, to notice the empty wine bottle on the nightstand, the glasses, one with wine still standing. On the vanity, a mirror was powdered with white and accented by a razor blade. A box of Trojans stood open beside it, with two torn wrappers on the floor beside the bed.

As Christal stepped closer, she could see that Manuel de Clerk was crying, his chest rising and falling with the sobs. Tears trickled down his sweat-slick cheeks. When he looked her way, it was with abject terror.

"She cut me!" he cried. "God, help me! Call an ambulance."

Christal stopped short. Each wrist and ankle had been tied off to one of the sturdy bed posts with a white nylon rope. His black pubic hair glistened, damp and matted. She winced at the dark red stain that had formed between the man's muscular thighs. As she watched, another drop of blood fell from the tip of de Clerk's limp penis.

# CHAPTER 35

When the light turned green, Lymon toed the gearshift into first. The transmission made a metallic clunk, and the big Indian rumbled and shook as Lymon eased the clutch out and accelerated. He rolled the throttle, letting all sixteen hundred and thirty-eight ccs bellow. The Indian wasn't loud—Lymon hated loud pipes—but it had an authoritarian rumble that sent a tingle up his spine.

The lights on Santa Monica Boulevard seemed to pulse with brighter than usual color. Or was that just part of the high that came out of a nice night and being tuned to the bike and his passenger? He waved at people sitting in a sidewalk pizza place just because it was fun and they were watching him ride past.

Sheela must have liked it, too; she tightened her hold on his waist. He fought the urge to reach down with his left hand and pat her leg where it rested against his hip.

"We should do this every night," Sheela called over his shoulder.

"You've got a schedule. Rex would go into apoplectic seizures. You're worth millions. You've got to take care of all your minions."

"I thought a minyan was ten Jews?"

"If you happen to be orthodox, it's ten *male* Jews. But that's spelled different."

"Details!" she cried.

"That's where the Devil is."

He enjoyed her crystal laughter and found himself smiling. Using a handful of front brake, he hauled the Indian down for the next red, pulling in behind a Toyota and leaving himself a bike length for escape as he watched a sedan slow behind him. Only when he was satisfied the car had stopped did he shift into neutral and let the big V twin drop into its *rumpity rumpity* idle.

Sheela reached up and wrapped her arms around his chest. He could feel her as she hugged him. "Thank you, Lymon. I really needed this."

"Hey, it's fun," he answered, trying to keep his voice light. "It's what I do for relaxation."

The light changed, and he accelerated with the traffic. The tranny shifted with a positive click. He was intimately aware of Sheela's body moving with his. They might have been matched, a curiously symbiotic twin sharing the night, the wind, and the sound. Part of it was the Indian's saddle. It forced the passenger to sit close. On the BMW she had been back, pretty much self-supported against the tour pack.

Damn his hide! His whole body seemed to be quivering as if every nerve and muscle were aware of her. Even individual cells were howling out in primitive cognizance of the healthy female pressing against him.

*Face it, it's more than just your hormones.*

His brain was piqued, too. Sure, she was beautiful and probably laced with the kind of pheromones his receptors were perfectly geared for, but he liked her. Enjoyed her company. He always had, from the moment he had first taken an interview with her.

*It won't work!* he reminded himself sternly.

She was a public lady, a superstar in a world where crossing the lines wasn't allowed. The few who had tried it had ended up as burned wreckage, picked over by the press and left to decompose.

"What?" she asked past the wind. "Did you say something?"

"Not out loud."

Her laughter was throaty. "Yeah, I can hear your thoughts, Lymon. Scary, huh?"

"Not as scary as the thoughts I was just thinking."

"About me?"

"You *can* read my mind."

He turned his head just far enough to give her a sidelong look. That's how the magazines should have photographed her, like that, with excitement and deviltry bubbling in her eyes, a natural blush on her perfect cheeks, and a delighted smile.

*Dear God, I love you.*

The words came rolling out of his subconscious. Cowed, he returned his attention to the traffic.

If anything proved quantum uncertainty, Heisenberg, Schrodinger's cat, and chaos theory, it was LA drivers. Nothing could ever be predicted with any accuracy. Only the constantly wary survived. It was Darwin maxed to the tenth power. He had to concentrate on that. Whatever it took to keep his brain cells preoccupied with anything but the inevitability of biology.

"Now what are you thinking?"

"You can't tell?"

"Not at the moment."

"I'm knotting my brain with quantum physics."

"Why?"

"It's easier than Buddhism."

She seemed to consider that for a moment, then propped her chin on his shoulder and said, "I've been imagining left-handed tantra myself."

"What?"

"Ever read the *Kama sutra?* Not the modern picture books, but the original?"

"We're not having this conversation."

To save himself, he flipped on the turn signal, leaned into a right, and rolled the throttle, sure enough of the surface to scrape a floorboard and the center stand.

Sheela tightened her grip and let out a shriek of delight. As they rolled down Coldwater, he heard his cell phone ring.

Pulling over, he toed the bike into neutral and slipped the phone out of his pocket. He asked, "Yeah?" as he killed the bike, trying to hear.

*"Lymon?"* Christal's voice was muffled by the foam of his helmet. *"There's trouble. It's Copperhead."*

"Where are you?"

*"Manuel de Clerk's. The police are here."*

"I know where he lives. I've got to make a drop-off, then I'll be right there."

*"You might want to hurry."*

He thumbed *End and* winced as a low rider rumbled

past with deafening exhaust and even louder bass speakers blasting music so loud the decibels were cracking the metallic blue paint off the car's body.

"You heard?" Lymon asked.

"Everybody in the western United States heard. I hate *Tejano* when it rattles my teeth. So, what's the drop-off?"

"You. Before I ride over to Manny's."

"I heard Christal say it was Copperhead."

"Yeah. So?"

"So, I'm going."

"Sheela, I don't need—"

"Punch the starter button there on the handlebar. That's the red one just up from your thumb. That's it."

The Indian chugged, popped, and rumbled to life.

"You work for me, Lymon," Sheela added curtly. "Your objections are duly noted for the record. Christal, however, also works for me."

"Oh, yeah? Who signs her checks?"

"You do, with my approval. I want to see what's happening. It's important to me." She tightened her hold as he found a hole in the traffic and unleashed the big engine's massive acceleration.

Sheela whooped in delight, tightening her arms around his chest. Then she propped her chin on his shoulder again, saying, "Here's the way it lines out: You're driving this thing, Lymon, so you could take me home. It's your motorcycle, so I couldn't do anything about it. Then, once you'd dropped me off, I'd just have to drive over to Manny's myself."

He gave her that half glance again, just to make sure she wasn't kidding. "You would, wouldn't you?"

"Make it easier on both of us."

"You win," he relented, pulling into the left turn lane at Sunset.

As they waited at the light, she said in a soft voice, "Thank you, Lymon. You really are a sweetie, did you know?"

"Yeah. All sugar and honey, that's me." But his stomach was flipping like Simone Biles on the uneven bars.

# CHAPTER 36

"Good, it was weird!" Manuel de Clerk repeated in a half-panicked voice. He was sitting in one of the hulkingly plush leather chairs placed randomly in the great room downstairs. A white terry cloth bathrobe was wrapped around him and belted snugly at the waist. It covered his bandaged penis.

"Look, Mr. de Clerk," one of the cops was saying, "we don't know what we've got to go on. So, you've got a nick out of your dick? Big deal. Sometimes you play a little rough, shit happens. You know what I mean?"

Christal stood against the wall, arms crossed as she listened. The room contained a knot of officers, most killing time as they enjoyed a glance around Manny's opulently furnished house and considered the implications of the small wound to his most private. All but a few of them managed to keep from snickering out loud, but it was in each officer's eyes.

The cop shrugged. "You picked the lady up, you let her into your house. Maybe she snagged a tooth on your dick, huh? The thing we do have a problem with is the cocaine on your nightstand. Now, it's not much, but we can't just ignore that."

"My client doesn't have to address that at this time," Vincent Quill, Manny's lawyer, said from the side. He was a middle-aged man, balding. Dressed in a casual brown jacket and pressed cotton slacks, he looked like a friggin' lawyer. "Manny has already informed me that the woman brought the cocaine."

"The woman did?" The cop glanced at his companions, who shrugged.

"Hey, I told you." Manny dropped his head into his hands. "I just met her. She showed up at my table at lunch. Said her name was Lily Ann Gish. That she'd met me at a party at Bernard's. Didn't I remember her?"

"And you just invited her home?" the cop asked.

"Well, hey, she was..." He looked around, aware of the skepticism. "She was cool." It sounded really lame.

"So you let some woman you didn't know into your house. You let her tie you up for sex. Then you say she whipped out a little knife and cut off a piece of your dick. After that, she just got dressed and walked out?"

Manuel nodded sickly. "Yeah, that's it."

"End of story."

"End of story." He looked up. "But for the buzzer. The buzzer went off in her purse. She said, 'Sorry, Manny. Something's up. And it ain't you anymore.' And she reached in her purse, pulled out that little knife, and—" He swallowed hard. "I thought she was going to castrate me! You wouldn't believe the look in her eyes."

"Triumphant?" Christal asked from the side.

"Yeah, God." Manny was running his hands through his sweaty black hair. "I asked her what she was doing. Shit, I was scared, you know? She just smiled, grabbed me, and sliced a piece off."

"Then what?" Christal asked. "Think about it. What did she do with the piece?"

The cops were giving her questioning looks. She raised a hand, stalling any outburst.

"Weird." Manny looked up, a slight frown on his handsome face. "She dropped it into one of the rubbers. She took both of the used rubbers, knotted them, you know? Like tying them off. And flipped them into her purse."

"She took the used rubbers?" the cop asked, glancing at the recorder.

"Yeah. I was screaming, telling her to let me loose. She just got dressed, never looked back, and walked away."

"Did you hear the gunshots?" Christal asked.

"*Bang. Bang. Bang.*" Manny nodded. "Yeah."

Christal took a deep breath. Copperhead took a piece of Manny—and two used condoms. Chalk up another bizarre twist.

"Do you need me anymore?" Christal asked.

"We have your statement," the cop told her. "You'll have to fill out the paperwork if you still want to press charges against the woman."

"Yeah," Christal said woodenly. "The bitch was trying to kill me."

"Do you think you can prove that?" Manny's lawyer asked unexpectedly.

Christal stared at him. "Granted, I'm new here, and as people have been reminding me, LA isn't the East Coast. But doesn't the discharge of a weapon when it's pointed in the direction of a fleeing human being indicate intent to you?"

The lawyer watched her flatly as Christal walked out of the room, found the front door, and stepped out into the night. She took a deep breath of the cool air and realized that a small crowd had gathered in the drive. Most were police; others, she suspected, were Manuel de Clerk's staff: managers, publicists, and the rest of the cadre that A-list stars seemed to require. Three guys she immediately recognized as security were standing on the other side of the yellow tape, looking particularly sheepish.

At the corner of the house, two of the crime scene specialists were looking for bullet holes in the weeping willow's thick bole. Evidently, Gretchen-Mouse hadn't dropped any of her spent brass.

"Christal!"

She raised her eyes, seeing Lymon and Sheela standing off to one side beside a big-fendered motorcycle. She pursed her lips and descended the steps before walking along the edge of the drive to the tape. She nodded at the cop there, ducked it, and walked over to where Lymon and Sheela waited.

"What the hell happened in there?" Lymon gestured at the house.

"How'd you get this far?"

Lymon grinned. "Connections with the department. That, and having an employee as a material witness helps."

Christal related the entire story, glancing curiously at Sheela when she got to the part about Copperhead. Sheela fixed on it like a terrier on a rat.

"Jesus," Lymon wondered. "She cut off Manny's dick and—"

"A small piece of foreskin actually," Christal corrected. "It bled like sixty, but the guy will hardly have a scar once it heals. The nutty thing is, she took two used condoms. What do you do with two used condoms? The sperm dies when the temperature drops."

"Souvenir?" Sheela asked as if she didn't believe it.

"Witch," Christal blurted, hardly aware she'd spoken.

"Ah, here we go again." Lymon lifted an eyebrow. "We're back to broomsticks and black cats."

Christal flashed a self-conscious smile. "As in take a piece of your victim to focus the evil on his body or soul." She shook it off. "It's nothing. Tales of my childhood."

"Mouse shot at you?" Sheela stepped closer, worry on her face. "Are you sure you're all right?"

Christal shrugged. "Hey, it was the first time. Shots in anger and all that. God, Lymon, if I'd had my pistol with me, I might have brought this whole thing to a conclusion."

"Killing Mouse would have landed you in a pile of shit." Lymon pointed a hard finger at her. "Don't even *think* it!"

"I wouldn't have killed her. Not if I could help it. Hey, I maxed the qualification. They were talking about the FBI pistol team. Maybe even the national pistol championship at Camp Perry. If I could have anchored Mouse, taken out two of the Audi's tires, we'd have them."

"You'd have what? A gunfight over stolen rubbers and a tampon?" Lymon gestured with his hands. "Christal, this isn't the Bureau. We're *not* a law enforcement agency. Are you getting this wedged into your hard little head? We provide security...protection. Period! We don't take offensive actions. If you can't begin to think in terms of cover and evacuate instead of attack and subdue, you're going to have to look for another line of work."

Christal winced at the censure in his voice. "Yes, sir."

Sheela stepped close, taking her arm. "It's all right. You've done a super job so far, Christal."

"Have I?" she asked bitterly. "Doing what? Copperhead's still a jump ahead of us." She cocked her head, hearing the voices whispering from her subconscious.

"What?" Lymon read her sudden confusion.

"I don't believe in witchcraft, do I?"

"Why would you ask that?" Sheela was watching her, a faint frown on her smooth brow.

"I don't know. But something clicked somewhere. I'll let you know as soon as I figure out what it is." Yes, she could sense that she was on the verge of making the connection.

"Are you ready to head for the barn?" Lymon asked.

Christal gave him a deadpan glare. "Sorry, boss. I've got to make an appearance at the station to file a complaint. I have paperwork to do."

"Pressing charges?"

"I'm going to be running into them again." Christal raised her arms in surrender. "And you're right. I heard you. We're not the cops. But, Lymon, if something goes wrong, I want it on the record that, one, there was trouble, and two, they were the aggravating party."

"It was probably just coincidence that they were here." Sheela didn't sound sincere. "In the weeks ahead, we'll all wonder what happened to them, what it was all about."

"No, I'll be seeing them again." Christal squinted into the darkness. She studied the bright lights at the end of the drive. The press was waiting like hungry lions. "Trust me. I can feel it."

# CHAPTER 37

The place was called Dusty Stewart's Santa Fe Grill. Christal had seen the sign as she drove down Sunset Boulevard and thought it was worth a try. Now she watched as the waitress placed a heaping plate in front of her. She thanked the woman and picked up her fork as she studied the steaming meal. The odor of corn tortillas and cumin had her salivating as she reached for the side of diced jalapeno peppers. She scooped them out over the enchiladas, creating a pattern of green accents on the melted yellow cheddar and red chili sauce.

The sounds of the restaurant covered Lymon's approach as he walked up, pulled out a chair, and plopped himself down beside her. He was wearing a brown blazer, sharply creased cotton pants, and a professional button-down shirt with a tan tie. His craggy face was creased with a smile, and his sandy hair looked unkempt.

"Good evening," he greeted, rearranging his blue paper napkin with its silverware. He glanced around at the pinatas, guitars, and Mexican pottery that decorated the painted stucco walls. Diluted strains of mariachi drifted down from the speakers, competing with the clatter of plates and the mumble of conversation.

"Hi, boss." Christal reached for the El Yucateco sauce in the centerpiece.

"You get a good day's sleep?" He gave the waitress a high sign. A Latina wearing a frilly white blouse, low cut, and a black Mexican-style wraparound skirt. "Smothered burrito," he told her, "and a Carta Blanca to drink."

Christal told him, "Yeah, I slept like a rock. Even when the yard crew was mowing the grass under my window. I finally woke up at five thirty." She made a face. "I think I'm turning into a bat."

"Glad to see you're breaking into the job. The schedule can take over your entire life." He hesitated. "Did you get my message?"

"That we're leaving for New York at midnight? That's for real?"

"Yep."

"This is kind of last-minute, isn't it?"

"It's the way Hollywood works. The bigwigs at the studio want Sheela to attend a preem in New York. Her presence will bring certain benefits to the studio. Ergo, we leave at midnight."

"What's a preem?"

"A premiere showing of a new movie. It's a publicity thing where they bring in all the stars, the director, the producers, and lots of the film critics. The idea is to butter up the critics with hype, let them get chummy with the actors, and they'll write a good review of your movie."

"Right. Why am I going? I'm the new kid on the block."

"Because whatever it is that you're doing, you're kicking results out of the weeds. Maybe you'll see something in New York that we'd miss."

She poked her fork into her enchilada. "Excuse me, I'm starting my breakfast." She took a taste and nodded. "Not bad."

He glanced around. "You can never tell about Mexican."

"Sure you can." Christal gestured with her fork. "Call ahead. If they have fresh jalapenos—like right off the bush—you're usually safe. If they say they have them in the cans, pickled, blow it off."

"That's the truth? Really?"

"Trust me. I'm one of the few New Mexicans who survived DC gustatorily unscathed."

He watched her just long enough to make her nervous. "Yes, boss? You want to ask me something?"

"You're from New Mexico."

"Born and bred. Who knows how many generations? I'm pure one hundred percent Southwestern mongrel: *Indio, Mexicano,* and Anglo all rolled into one."

He indicated her enchiladas. "Not everyone can eat that stuff with fresh peppers like that."

"Does this have a point?"

"Tell me more about your grandmother."

That stopped her short. "Why on earth would you ask about her?"

"You said she was a witch."

"Grandma was a *curandera,* a healer. Not a witch." She paused. "Well, okay...*maybe* not a witch. She was into the old folk remedies. You know, herbs for pains and aches. Taking sweat baths to purge evils from the blood. And, well, sometimes some things that were a little off the wall for the twentieth century, let alone the twenty-first."

"Such as?"

"She cured a guy of stomach cancer once." Christal balanced her fork in emphasis. "The doctors in Albuquerque told the guy that the cancer was Stage Advanced Four. Told him to just go home and die. He didn't have anything left, so he came wandering up to Grandma's house one day. She lived in a little adobe off the road on the way up to Nambe. Had a garden, a ramada, the whole bit."

"And she cured him?"

Christal chewed, took a swig of her Coke, and shrugged. "The guy was a walking scarecrow—brown skin over bones. You kind of expected him to snap in two at a loud noise. But getting back to the story, Grandma did some things. I didn't understand the what or why of them. She walked around him, chanting in the old tongue, shaking a rattle and swatting him with a wand she'd made of sage, chamisa, and manzanita. She made him swallow some kind of concoction she'd brewed and sent him home."

"And that cured him?"

"No, she told him to eat rattlesnake."

"Rattlesnake?"

"Yep. And the guy did. He was all over that country looking for rattlesnakes. Offered twenty dollars apiece for them. I guess he ate rattlesnake fried, broiled and boiled, baked, fricasseed, smoked, steamed, microwaved, and every other way you could imagine."

Lymon made a face. "And *that* cured him?"

"He was still alive five years later. What the cancer failed to do, a Ford truck did. He was hit on his bicycle one Friday night by some kids who had been swigging their beer in quarts."

She arched a challenging eyebrow. "The thing is, he'd gained weight, straightened out, and could ride all over the country on his bicycle. The physicians were mystified by his recovery. But for a pickup weaving out of its lane, who knows? He might still be pedaling around looking for rattlesnakes."

Lymon said nothing as his food arrived. He sipped his beer, then picked up his fork. "Did they do an autopsy?"

"What for? Cause of death was pretty straightfor-ward. The guy had the letters *F-O-R-D* stamped into his chest."

Lymon gave her an amused look. "What about this witch stuff?"

"*Some* people called her a witch," Christal corrected. "It depended on if she liked you or not. Truth is, at times she scared the living bejesus out of me. The upper Rio Grande country is a funny part of the world, and Grandma was old school. I think she considered the 1846 American occupation of New Mexico as a passing inconvenience."

"So, why did you think of Copperhead as a witch last night?"

Christal scraped up a forkful of *refritos*. "I've been wondering that myself."

She chewed for a while. "It's nothing I can say outright. I mean, these celeb hits, they're after a piece of the person. Does that mean I think that Copperhead and Mouse are locked away in some basement apartment, drawing pentagrams on the floor and repeating spells from *The Necronomicon*? No."

"So, what? What can a person do with Sheela's tampon?"

"Or a slip of de Clerk's foreskin?" She shrugged. "I don't know. They took Talia Roberts's sheets and garbage. Someone nabbed Bullock's dirty hankies; Gibson lost the head of his razor. Those things are different than a small patch of foreskin."

"Are they?" Lymon hacked off a forkful of burrito.

"Bed linen isn't in the same league as part of a man's most precious."

"The press is all over this. The studio canceled shooting today." Lymon sipped his beer. "Manny is said to be a little distraught."

"If you think he's distraught now, you should have seen him staked out on that bed." She paused. "What are we missing here? They keep getting pieces of men. John Lennon's hair, Manny's foreskin, Mel Gibson's razor scuzz. With women, it's sheets, tissues, tampons, toothbrushes, hairbrushes, and fluids."

"It can't be to turn a buck. The bad guys walked right past a lot of stuff that would have fenced for a bundle."

"You know, Lymon, they're taking the kind of stuff that crime scene guys consider pure gold: DNA, HLA, hairs, blood type, fibers, lots of things."

"So, maybe it's DNA?"

"Sure, maybe. But that doesn't make sense."

"Why is that, Sherlock?"

"If it was DNA, why would they be involved in these high-profile assaults and burglaries? Do you know how easy it is to get someone's DNA? They could have done something as facile as grabbing Sheela's champagne flute at the Wilshire."

"Her champagne flute? How?"

"They could have isolated a couple of mesodermal cells from the lipstick smudge she left on the rim. Or, better, someone could have grabbed the paper towel she'd dried her hands on after she threw it in the trash. They didn't need to set up an elaborate hoax with fake legs and a plastic-lined toilet. In Talia Roberts' case, they didn't need to take the sheets. Cops pull DNA off of sticky-tape samples that pick up flakes of skin."

"But these aren't cops."

"No," Christal mused. "But if they *were* after DNA, they'd know how simple it is to get it."

"Okay, so DNA's out." He paused. "What would a witch want with any of this stuff?"

"You know how they give bloodhounds an article of clothing so they can track down the person? Evil magic works the same way. A witch needs to have something very personal and intimate to tie the curse to. Like an email address to direct the evil to the right person."

"You know"—he gave her a level look—"I don't buy this witchcraft stuff."

"Neither do I. Despite my upbringing."

"Then, why are you looking so worried?"

"Because it's not what you or I believe that's at issue."

"Okay, I'll bite. Why?"

She gave him a grim smile. "Because all that matters is that someone *does* believe it. Figure out that core belief and this whole thing will make perfect sense."

He considered that. "Just like the stalkers. At least

one in particular. I told you about her. She believes that Sheela is secretly in love with her."

"Krissy, right?"

"Right."

"Then you begin to understand."

"But that's a delusion. An obsession gone wrong. An example of the human brain making up rules when it operates dysfunctionally."

"And witchcraft isn't?"

"Hell, I don't know."

They ate in silence. Finally, Lymon put his fork down. "Here's the thing: The guy in New York didn't look like a wacko."

"What did he look like?"

"Like a professional...doing a job."

"Yeah," she mumbled. "Just like Copperhead."

"So much for your theory."

Christal crunched a jalapeno between her teeth, savoring the burst of flavor. "Maybe not witchcraft, Lymon. But something similar, something parallel." She frowned. "And I'm going to figure it out and bring it to a stop no matter what it takes."

# END OF ATHENA UNLEASHED

## PART ONE OF THE ATHENA TRILOGY

We hope you have enjoyed the first part of The Athena Trilogy.

Part Two, *Genesis Athena*, continues the story as dark and deadly forces close in on Sheela, Christal, and Lymon. Available soon for download or in paperback from your favorite bookseller.

And finally, we hope you enjoy Part Three, *Athena's Wrath*, as Sheela takes matters into her own hands in an attempt to uncover a terrible and shocking secret. But after suffering the ultimate betrayal, she will discover that nothing comes without a horrendous cost, and the price will be paid in blood.

# A LOOK AT BOOK TWO:
## GENESIS ATHENA

**Taken from today's headlines and insidiously prophetic, part two in the evocative and acclaimed Athena Trilogy will have you questioning the boundaries of morality and the sordid depths of today's celebrity obsession.**

As the eerie game of cat and mouse between the shadowy organization, Genesis Athena, and Hollywood diva, Sheela Marks, grows more sinister by the day, the stakes are raised and the walls close in.

Desperate to protect Sheela, Bodyguard Lymon Bridges turns to disgraced FBI Agent Christal Anaya. Peeling away layers of deceit and secrecy, Christal's determined to uncover why celebrity DNA is being stolen in high-profile assaults and break-ins. But just as she's closing in on the sordid truth, her former FBI partner resurfaces, hell-bent on stopping her—even if it means drugging and abducting her.

Sheela knows it's up to her to save Christal and expose Genesis Athena and its sinister mastermind. But to do so, she will have to give the performance of her lifetime, which begs the question: who is Sheela, really, and what is she capable of?

***Stunningly dark and eerily prophetic, Genesis Athena is an unnerving story of obsession, peril...and chilling possibilities.***

*AVAILABLE FEBRUARY 2024*

# About the Author

**W. Michael Gear** is a *New York Times, USA Today,* and international bestselling author of sixty novels. With close to eighteen million copies of his books in print worldwide, his work has been translated into twenty-nine languages.

Gear has been inducted into the Western Writers Hall of Fame and the Colorado Authors' Hall of Fame—as well as won the Owen Wister Award, the Golden Spur Award, and the International Book Award for both Science Fiction and Action Suspense Fiction. He is also the recipient of the Frank Waters Award for lifetime contributions to Western writing.

Gear's work, inspired by anthropology and archaeology, is multilayered and has been called compelling, insidiously realistic, and masterful. Currently, he lives in northwestern Wyoming with his award-winning wife and co-author, Kathleen O'Neal Gear, and a charming sheltie named, Jake.

Made in the USA
Coppell, TX
02 May 2024

31952429R00150